Heart

Be

Still

A Novel By
Aisha Buford-Morrison

HEART BE STILL

This novel is a work of fiction. Any resemblances to real people, living or dead, actual events, establishments, organizations, or locales are intended to give the fiction a sense of reality. Other names, characters, places, and incidents are either products of the author's imagination or are used fictitiously.

Author: Aisha Buford-Morrison
ISBN-13: 978-0692073957
ISBN-10: 0692073957
LCCN: TBD
Editing/Typesetting/Bookcover: Young Dreams Publications

Connect with Aisha Buford-Morrison

theauthoraisha@gmail.com

Twitter: @theauthoraisha

Instagram: theauthoraisha

Dedications

To my darling and beautiful, Mother, thank you for putting all your energy into raising me. I truly do love you and I am so proud to be your daughter. Thank you, God, for blessing me with the gift of being able to write.

Acknowledgements

Over 50,000 words, 3 ½ years of hard work, thank you for making this young 19-year-old, African American female from the South Side of Chicago the happiest person on the planet. This was all but a dream. Life is a never-ending story, every time you think the story has ended a new page appears.

Preface

This novel, *Heart Be Still*, was written from a dream I had for 3 ½ years straight. This novel is to show people that no matter the situation you have been through love will always shine through. We all experience hard times no matter how little or small. Each and every last chapter in our lives is presented with an issue that has to be solved. Some chapters are presented with issues more severe than the others. This book showcases the struggles of life, but most importantly the overall growth through the struggles. All of the situations presented shows that you cannot achieve greatness without pain and growth. I believe that everyone will be able to relate to this book one way or another. I'm forever grateful to be able to have this opportunity. Thank You.

~Aisha

AISHA BUFORD-MORRISON

Born During an Earthquake

I often wonder how much can a person take. Or what someone's breaking point is. And once they reach that breaking point and lose their minds, how much damage can a person do? I can't even imagine it. I really want to know the answer to this question but I don't know how or where to find the answer. I search my own situation to determine how much the human body can take of being pushed, kicked, and shoved around before it breaks. Why take the risk of losing the ones we love to our own selfishness? I feel like my life is a mess. My world is falling apart and I don't know how to fix it. My mom and dad are fighting again - that's nothing new. Being in this house I feel like I'm living in a mental institution. I need a break from the chaos but don't know how to escape it.

I don't think my parents realize how much it hurts to see them fight every single day. It's hard seeing your parents' marriage fall apart right before your eyes and there is nothing you can do about it. My parents were friends for years before they got married. They used to play with each other as kids. I can't seem to figure

1

out exactly where it all went wrong for them. My parents used to love each other. We used to be a normal family.

"Aquila, you can eat." Mom says yelling up to my room from the kitchen.

"I'll eat later, Mom. Thanks. I have a lot of homework to do." I says hoping she would leave me alone. I wanted to eat later when they both were asleep. You know, enjoy the peace and quiet.

"Aquila, get your ass down here and eat. I'm not going to argue with you tonight!" Mom yells.

"Mika, would you stop yelling at her. If she wants to stay in her room let her. She probably has homework to do." I can hear my dad yell out to my mom.

"Don't tell me how to raise my daughter!" Mom quickly spat back at him. "Aquila, I said now, and I mean right now!" She shouts back at me.

"She's my daughter, too!" He yells back at her. Dad was in a constant battle of getting his points heard to my mom. I could tell by his tone of voice he was getting angrier as they talk.

"Since when have you ever given a damn? I have done all of the heavy lifting in raising her." Mom says matter-of-factly.

 2

"I have always cared about her!" He yells.

"No, you have not. You know what? I'm not talking about this!" As soon as my mom sees me coming down the stairs she abruptly ends the argument.

Hearing that the argument was about me I decide that I didn't want to be the fuel to yet another one of their arguments. Coming down stairs and sucking it up was my only hope of stopping the bickering. I tell myself to just get my plate, sit down, and shut up. It was very awkward sitting there, all at the dinner table as if we were some happy family, especially after my parents were just chewing each other's' heads off. I was just hoping that we could eat quickly before another argument got to brewing.

As we sat there eating our dinner no one looks at each other, only down at our plates as we eat in weird silence. Sometimes I wish that they would just get a divorce and be done with it already. The constant fighting was breaking up our once happy home. Fighting would break out over the simplest thing that in a normal house would never be an issue. It was always a waiting game to see what would spark the fireworks between the two of them. Right before dinner it was about me not coming down stairs. Who knows, any second it could be over one of them not passing the salt nicely… you just never know with them.

I eat my dinner in a hurry to get back to my room before they start arguing again. This house was an insane asylum and I couldn't catch a break for nothing. I mean, I loved my parents, but damn just sign the divorce papers already. I'm sick of this! I don't think they even recognize how this affects me and my future relationships.

I quickly rush up to my room and lie down in my bed staring at the ceiling. In the quietness of my room I think about everything. It was getting pretty late I knew I needed to be getting to bed, but all I could think about was if I should speak to my parents about how their arguing was bothering me. I wonder if my voice would really make a difference to them. But I was scared to say anything because I knew I would get my ass kicked. And it also didn't help that I have both of their tempers in me so I might not say things correctly. I see now why they called me the 'devil's child' when I was growing up. I hope the way my parents are acting is not a glimpse of how I will act in my adult life. I don't want to be fighting with my husband while my child is upstairs locked away suffering trying to find a way out.

The only person who knows what my life is like is Kiowa, I call him Ki for short. He has been my best friend since the dawn of time. I feel he is the only one who can understand me. I want to call him but it was late so I decide I would wait until the next day to talk to him. I was hoping that he could give me some answers on what the hell to do. Kiowa has been my confidant and I was happy that I was able to confide in him with what was going on in my life because I had no one else I could really talk to. Although I did have other friends I've come to learn that everyone doesn't understand how to comfort you in your life. Most of the time Ki thinks I should talk to my dad, but most times I don't really like my dad.

My dad is just... well he's something alright. He works at the police station and saves people every day. I believe he chooses to work long hours so he does not have to come home. The long hours is not so bad but what he chooses to do after work. Instead of coming home to his wife and child he chooses to go hang out with his friends. I should be used to him doing that because he's been doing that for years – but I realize that it still bothers me because I'm still waiting on him to change. So I've chosen to reduce myself to only say about two words to him every day. Sometimes I just want to run away from it all, and make my entire problem go away. There have been times when I tried to plan it out, but I quickly would change my mind. I knew that he would send the whole army to find me. Yet again I still think he is a bit of a jackass. I go back and forth with it sometimes. I hate him sometimes and then other times I love him, honestly it just depends on how I'm feeling at the moment.

Dealing with my parents I feel lost sometimes. I often feel stuck in the middle and end up being on my mom's side. I'm the child in the situation but I feel confused and frustrated because I keep trying to figure out where all the fighting is come from. I know for a fact that it is something that they are not telling me and that makes me upset because I hate not knowing important things. I live in the same house with the fighting so at least they can let me in on what's causing the disarray. I hope they can make up because I don't know how much more I can take of this. All I can do is hope for the better and pray the worst stays away. I want my parents to grow old together and be happy, but right now that seems impossible. I want them to be in the same room without fighting over everything. I feel like everything is going to go wrong. I have no clue to how I'm going to help them put the pieces back together. The issue is that they're both too busy with work to deal with their marital problems.

My mom opened her own store, Waters, here in Ruben right after we moved off the Reservation when I was about two years old. Ruben was a small town in the middle of nowhere and everyone here knows each other. Even though we don't live on the Reservation anymore Ruben is sort of like living on the Reservation. Most people who live in Ruben are Native Americans. I'm proud of my heritage, it's important for me to be able to keep my Native roots. I want to make sure that I pay respect to those who have come before me. Though they're gone they will never be forgotten, their blood still runs through my veins.

Waters is a good distraction for my mother, but not for me. She works me like a horse after school. She knows this is my last year of high school and that I just want to chill. But I realize that just because it's my last year of school does not mean she's going to take it easy on me, if anything she'll work me harder because I'll be entering into the real workforce and college soon after I graduate.

I need to talk to Ki so that I could dump all my feelings on him because I know he'll understand where I am coming from. His parents split up a few years ago, so I know he'll have some great advice for me to take. Soon after my mind slowed down and I was able to stop stressing about my parents and I eventually fall asleep.

Due to the stress of my life my dreams have begun to become very vivid over the last year. This particular night I had a dream that I believe was giving me clues to what will happen next in my life. The dream was kind of weird because I saw myself dying, but right before I take my last breath I always wake up. I wonder if seeing your own death is weird or not? Yeah, that's weird and I'm struggling to find out what it all really means. I have been having this same dream for months and I think it is a sign or a clue to something… or maybe I'm just crazy. Could it mean that someone else was going to die in my place? I couldn't figure out what the dream meant. Maybe it's my subconscious. Maybe I feel like if I disappeared that all my problems will vanish away. Why do we always want to run away from our problems instead of facing them? The next day can't come any sooner because Ki was good at helping me figure things out. And it was about time that I told him about the dreams I was having because they were eating away at me.

I know I'm going on and on about my parents, but when it comes to them sometimes I feel that they hate each other because of me. But then again a part of me says that I couldn't possibly be the reason for their hatred toward one another. I just go back and forth with this in my mind because I go right back to believing that they actually do hate me because it's always because of me that they're fighting. The situation is consuming my thoughts and I can't seem to get from under them. Some things in my life just don't make sense anymore.

Understand that I'm speaking from the mind of a child coming from a dysfunctional broken home. I don't know what to do anymore. It's like I'm lost at sea. I need to find a way that could lead to my survival, but I don't know how. The frustrating part about this is knowing that there's no way out of this mess that is my life – at least the part that I control. I keep telling myself to find a happy place. Or maybe I could start taking drugs so I can be loopy and carefree… forget I even mentioned that, it was just a reckless thought. I'm trying to process things as rationally as I could possibly do in my immature mind.

I have not even told Taika about what's going on. I mean how can you not tell your boyfriend what's going on? We haven't been together that long. He is my first boyfriend and I'm sort of new to this so I get confused on what I should confide in him about and what should just be between Ki and me. But I thought boyfriends were supposed to be the ones who you want to hold you when you're sad. The person you want to kill when they piss you the hell off. I don't know… this boyfriend thing is not going exactly the way I thought it should. Taika really wants to meet my parents but I don't think that's such a good idea. I also haven't met his mom.

I'm just hesitant about him meeting my parents because it is embarrassing with all their fighting. I don't even want to see it, so I can imagine how he would feel to see them fighting. He just does not need to see that part of them. Ki knowing about my parents is good enough.

Kiowa always helps me out when I need him to and I do the same for him in return. When I and Taika go through what Ki likes to call our "theater bullshit", he always offers to beat Taika up for me. I think it's funny sometimes. It's unfortunate that they don't get along. It would've been nice if the two important men in my life were friends. Kiowa is very protective over me and lately it's been getting worst. He says it's nothing but him being a good friend. I have been questioning that a lot lately. He's starting to argue and fight with Taika for every little thing and they are both working my nerves to be honest.

There's also been so much stuff going on with Kiowa. He's been acting strange lately. I'm starting to get very worried about him. He doesn't seem like his head's all together - like his mind is in another place. He has been fighting with everyone lately. Just last week he made our English teacher cry. I tried asking him about it but he says he can't tell me what has been going on. I find this a bit unnerving because we tell each other everything. I feel some type of way that he won't let me in on what's bothering him.

It's becoming exhausting having to keep telling him to calm down and being the referee when he gets a little out of hand. I guess we are both having troubles. Senior year is proving to be one of the most stressful years I have ever had. Hopefully we can get through this year together and make it out without too many scratches and bruises.

As I wake up early at 5:30 I'm say a silent prayer optimistic that today would be better than tomorrow. But I don't know because the day feels weird. I still had the thought of the dream looming over my head and plus it feels like there is going to be a big change in my life. Don't ask me where that feeling came from it just washed over me out of nowhere. Maybe I'm being hopeful that my parents will finally start working things out. Or maybe it really was just the stress about college and my parents, but I was for sure feeling that there was going to be a major change. I think it's a warning of some sorts, maybe I'm losing it.

It takes me about three hours every day to get out the door for school. In the midst of that I always end up spending unnecessary time trying to stop my parents from arguing with each other. I just want to hurry and get to school so I can get my mind off them. School is somewhat of break until I see them in the evening for dinner. But I'm happy that it's Wednesday. I always look forward to Wednesdays because that is our family night that we go out to eat. This is somewhat of a break from all the madness. They don't argue in public because it makes them look bad, and one thing my mother and father are good at is keeping up appearances.

When I finally get to school Kiowa is standing right by my locker like any other day. He says he meets me at my looker because it always seems to put a smile on my face, and it does. But today something is off with him. He looks kind of mad I immediately wonder what's going on.

"Hey, Ki. What's wrong?" I ask.

"Nothing. Why do you say that?" He smiles showing off his pearly white teeth.

"You look pissed, that's why. Are you OK? You really think after knowing you all these years I can't tell when you're upset?" I laugh at him.

"Yeah, I'm fine. What's up with you?" He asks.

"The same thing as always." I say putting my book bag in my locker.

"What was the argument this time? The last couple of arguments have been getting worse." He says looking at me knowing already what I've been through that morning.

"It was over me again and my dad working late. Look I really don't want to talk about them. I get to have a peacefully dinner tonight." I say sarcastically.

"Damn! It's Wednesday! Shit, I did not study for pre-cal!" Ki says upset trying to figure out what to do.

"We sit by each other just copy what I write down. Just know that you owe me." I tell him with a calm tone. The bell cuts off Kiowa when he was going to say thank you. But he didn't have to say it aloud, his eyes says it for him.

While I was walking to class Taika sees me. I have been trying to avoid him. We got into this big fight the other day and we have not made up yet. I'm not in good spirits today with the way my morning went, so I'm not in the mood to try to make up with him. I quickly dip off down the opposite hallway to get to English class. I must see him at lunch, I'll deal with him then.

I'm sitting in pre-calculus bored out of my mind. This class is very easy to me. Actually, I've never really had any problems in math, my grades are always high and I manage to ace every test. I'm watching the clock waiting on the bell to ring for next period. I'm also waiting on Ki to kick my foot to let me know he's done so I can turn my test in. Four classes in and I just want the day to be over with. I'm happy I have lunch next because I'm starving to death, but I'm dreading to see Taika. Ki finally finishes copying answers and just as I'm laying my paper on my teacher's desk the bell rings for lunch.

"Thanks again, Quil! I owe you. You ready to go to lunch?" Ki says as we walk down the hall.

"Yeah, I'm starving." I smile.

I hate walking through the hallways. It seems that everyone's in a rush to either get to their next class or go to the media center to pick up papers. I think I'm just being grouchy because I have too much going on in my personal life. When Kiowa and I finally get to the lunch room the line is wrapped around the corner - damn near outside the cafeteria. I'm so happy I bring my own lunch it saves time. I spot Ayana and Lilly and head over their way so we can goof off a bit before we stuff our faces. Ayana is Taika's younger sister by nine months and Lily and I have been good friends since grammar school. As I'm walking up to the lunch table I spot Taika. I immediately wish I could turn around and skip lunch, but I must face the music.

"Hey, Aquila, these are for you." Taika says as he attempts to hand me the flowers. The flowers were actually beautiful. It was as if I was a lion and he was handing me a piece of meat so I would play nice with him.

"Flowers? How… how thoughtful of you." I quickly grab the flowers out of his hand. "Look, I don't want to talk about what happened. I'm really not in the mood today for any of this." I look at him with utter disgust.

"So that means I'm off the hook, right?" He says looking at me with puppy dogs eyes. "I am truly sorry." He says happily with a stupid grin on his face. This only made me want to slap the shit out of him.

"No! I don't want to talk about the fact that you don't respect me, and I'm not taking these flowers!" I roll my eyes and throw them back at him.

"I'm sorry I called you a worthless bitch and that I can get a better girl than you. I was just mad. I tend to be a child when I'm upset." His effort to be cute and sweet fail. His condescending tone was making me question why I put up with him.

"Whatever, Taika! You should be thanking me. I talked Kiowa out of beating your ass. You know how he is with me." I turn away from him.

I sit down at the table with the girls breaking into the already going conversation. Everyone has pretty much finished the school year in their heads and we were all just ready to graduate. Everyone was dreading the twenty-page paper we must do to meet qualifications for graduation. The assignment was to write about our thoughts on Native American history and its impact on American history. Our friend, Josh, seems to think twenty pages is a slap in the face to the culture. He seems to believe that everyone has more than twenty pages of words to say about the culture.

"How the hell are we going to write a twenty-page paper on our culture? You know how many stories we have heard about our ancestors in our young lives? The topic doesn't require twenty pages!" He continues his rant passionately while eating his food.

"If I'm able to do my best impression of you Josh your paper sounds like this, the history of our people is simple. We lived free and normal lives until the Europeans came over and raped our women. They killed our children, brought smallpox's over which wiped out half of our people. Then we went to war and had a blood bath with the Europeans, they gave us a small piece of land that wasn't even where the tribes lived back then. And fast forward to current America, over some five-hundred years later, they're still trying to take our land from us. Then once a year on Halloween they decide that it's OK to use our cultural clothing to wear as costumes as they continually rape our culture for no reason.

Sounds about right?" I stand up looking him his eyes as I was going to throw away my trash.

"Ha, ha, very funny, Aquila. And you're right, that is how my paper is going to sound – just with much more factual details because everything you just said is true. Your version was just more short and to the point." He fake laughs and winks his eyes chewing on his burger.

For most of us it's an easy paper because we don't have to do much research on history. For most of the students seeing that many of their grandparents are still alive and have very vivid memories of the stories that have been passed down through the generations. Most of the school students' are towns people, however, at the end of the school after we've busted our butts for four years no one wants to write a twenty page paper, except for Josh.

After that awkward and amusing lunch it was time for study period. I liked this period, it gives me a chance to write and be free of listening to my teachers talk for forty-five minutes. Today was different I had nothing on my mind. I had a serious case of writer's block and I had nothing to write on my paper. I must have stared at that paper for the whole period because the next thing I knew it was time to go and off to two more classes.

Finally, after seven long hours of school it was time for me to go home - which honestly was the last place I wanted to be. Yeah, it was Wednesday and we were going out to eat, but that didn't mean that I wasn't going to be subject to an argument before we got to the peaceful dinner. When I got home my mom was already waiting on me. I went to my room like usual and changed my clothes then came back down stairs while mom and I waited for my dad. When dad eventually comes through the door, of course there was an argument because dad was a little late. He was only like three minutes late. Like really three minutes! I couldn't believe my mom was making such a big deal out of it. I found it helpful to just put on my headphones to drown out some of the noise.

Peace and quiet! Thank you! Is what I say to myself as we sit down and look over our menus to see what we were going to eat for the night. I enjoyed eating at Sal's, it was an old restaurant but felt cozy and inviting. It's been around for a century and has all these old artifacts that you can't find anywhere else in the world. I think of myself as an old soul sometimes. Some of the things that I find enjoyable most of my friends don't understand. Sometimes I feel like an old elderly lady because I enjoy talking to the older people than I do my friends at times. I can never get tired of this place. I don't even know why I bother to look over the menu. I always get the Hawaiian burger with fries and a shake, no matter what. Usually my parents just sit there questioning me about everything that is me and act like we are a family. Not tonight something was wrong I just can't figure out what, after that quiet dinner we head for home. And yup, you guessed it. My parents were arguing again. They were so angry with one another it was making me nervous.

"I can't believe you could do that in front of me! How on earth could you look at that woman's chest?" Mom screams at the top of her lungs.

"Mika, please I don't have time for your shit tonight." Dad responds back to her brushing her off carelessly.

"My shit, Rhys? My shit, Rhys? You know what? Fuck you!" She says and then begins to hit him.

Dad found it funny and decides to egg mom on some more. "If you did that more often I would not need to look at other women!" He sarcastically says making her more furious.

I thought my mom was going to burst a blood vessel the way she looks at him. I could not take it anymore. It was like a spirit had come over me and finally I let my parents know how I feel. I was not holding back on anything. I decide that I would deal with their punishment later, but now I had to let them know what was up. I take off my seat belt so I could get all in their face.

"Mom and dad!! For once in your goddamn life would you please stop arguing! I'm sick and tired of you two! Every day and every night you guys must argue every single day. For once just stop with your shit!! We are a broken family! Please do me a huge favor and get a divorce already! God! Nothing both of you do make sense anymore."

Mom and dad were stunned. They couldn't believe what I had said. Just as they were ready to lay into me for my foul mouth, my dad takes his eyes off the road for a spilt second. He was so distracted by me that he didn't see the grizzly bear crossing the road. Before I know it the car is spinning out of control and I am flying out of the front window. Just before I pass out all I hear are screams, the last thing I remember seeing was the car on fire.

The Realization

My mind is my prison and there is no key for me to get out.

After long nights of being held hostage to my thoughts I'm

consumed, trapped with no way out. It eats me alive until I choke

almost passing out.

"Aquila, wake up, please. Come on open your eyes. Can you hear me?" Kiowa says holding my hand.

I wake up feeling disoriented and to a bewildered looking Kiowa. The look on his face screams that something was wrong. For some reason I couldn't really see him, everything looks blurry, but I know the silhouette is him. I realize my arms were covered with different cords with bags attached to them. My whole body was in unbearable pain. I have tubes coming from everywhere, not to mention my right side was hurting so badly that I squirm in discomfort as I attempt to move. I can't figure out what was wrong. I didn't remember anything.

"Kiowa…" I try to speak louder but my voice was practically nonexistent.

"Do you need me to go get my mom?" Kiowa says ready to run and find her.

Soon I realize I was in the hospital. "Your mother's my doctor?" I say in a soft whisper very confused.

"That's the only way I found out you were here." Ki says grabbing my hand.

"Wait… Where are my parents? Are they OK?" I begin to panic with the thought of the accident rushing back to my memory suddenly.

"Aquila the accident was really bad. Quil, when the ambulance got there the car was on fire. You went through the windshield your mom told them to focus on you and not her. She gave her life for you. She told them to tell you that she loves you and they will be watching over you. I'm so sorry." Ki says in one breath trying to break the news to me all at once.

The pain I was feeling began to grow and along with it came and abundance of sadness and regret. I could not believe that Kiowa was telling me that they had left me here alone. The last thing we did was argue. I feel weak and unbalanced. I immediately go numb. My mind was blank and I could not believe that I was officially all alone in this world. I had lost my entire world in a split second. The tears began to flow like a fountain. I was overcome with so much grief I couldn't get control of myself. Kiowa did his best to get me to stop crying, but all I thought to myself was that the reason my parents were dead was my fault. What was I to do? I only wanted them to stop fighting. I never thought my outburst would result in their death. I want them back. I want to hear their voices and feel their presence in the room. I felt so lost without them.

Kiowa looked on helplessly until I finally cry myself to sleep. I'm not sure how long I was out, but I woke back up to Ki looking at me powerless as he was unable to comfort me or change the events of the day. We sit there in silence just looking at one another and then Ki's mom walks into the hospital room.

"Aquila, you're finally woke! My lovely patient." She says with a smile.

"Ms. Maddox, hi. How are you?" I say half-heartedly.

"The question is, dear, how are you? And I'm sorry for your loss. I know things are going to be hard for you for a minute, but I want you to know that everything will be fine. I'm here for you whatever you need." She expresses in sorrow.

"Um… ok." Realizing that I had bandages on my face I want to know when I could take them off. "Ms. Maddox, when can I take the bandages off my face? The seeing out one eye is not working." I feel guilty asking but I was uncomfortable.

"Right now they need to be changed, but they will have to go back on. This time we won't cover your eye. But Aquila before we do that, I must tell you that you suffered a lot of damage and blood loss. The right side of your body was cut badly from you being tossed out the window. I must prepare you for what you're going to see. Your face is not going to look the same." Ms. Maddox says cautiously.

After Ki's mom explained the situation my nerves became shot. I did not know what to expect my face to look like. She starts to cut the bandages off. I want to jump off the bed and run to a mirror. The anticipation was killing me more than the pain itself. The way she described it only made me feel worst. And now my mind was racing. What if I look like a cut up mess? What if I look ugly? I grip the sheets because the suspense was killing me. She finally gets all of the bandages off my face and the look on their faces has me worried. Kiowa's eyes widen so much I thought they were going to pop out of his head. Ms. Maddox looks at me with a blank stare on her face. I sit there waiting for them to say a word, but they only have blank looks on their faces. It was like they forgot how to form sentences. Ki was finally able to figure out how to put words together.

"I've never seen a person so beautiful in my life. You are absolutely gorgeous." Kiowa says with a big smile on his face.

"May I please see a mirror?" I ask because I knew he was full of shit.

"Aquila, dear, I don't think that's a good idea right now. Sweetie as of right now your face is swollen and has a lot of stitches in it. It looks worse than what it will look like once you're healed completely. I don't want you to freak out you have nothing to worry about." She says with compassion.

"Please just let me see. I have lost so much, please don't try and protect me from the truth." I begin to cry.

Ms. Maddox sends one of the nurses to go and find a mirror for me. She tries to make me feel better than what I was feeling. The skinny nurse creeps into the room and hands the mirror over to Kiowa's mom.

"Aquila, here's a mirror." She says hesitantly.

I grab the mirror ready for the moment of truth. I was so nervous the mirror almost slides out of my hands because my palms were so sweaty. I almost didn't want to look but I knew I had to. I put the mirror up to my face and I could not even believe what I see. I was cut up all over. I didn't even recognize my own face. The face I had seen every day when I woke up in the morning was now gone. I was crying yet again at the devastation – not only were my parents gone but it was clear I was going to be left with a reminder of it every single day I would look into the mirror. I look like something out of a horror movie. It was like I was not even in my own body and I became a stranger to my own self. The sadness that comes over my heart was like the clouds covering the sun and all I could do is cry everything out. I'm hurt and angry at everything.

My face looks like I was attacked by a wild animal. There was a huge scar starting from where my ear was to my nose. Then there were a lot of broken off scars that connected to the larger scar. My nose had a bunch of stitches in it which made it hard to breathe at times. There also was another gash on my forehead that hurts when I try and make any facial movements or expressions. My face is so swollen I could barely make out who I was – I was a total completely different person. I never thought I was the prettiest girl to begin with, but this was the only face I've seen for the last eighteen years – and now it was gone. Just yesterday I had big black eyes, a button nose, and clear skin. Looking in the mirror the only thing that remains the same way is my long black hair. Other than that I don't know who I am. I was bloody, bruised, and broken.

There's a lot going on with me that I can't even think straight, I just feel like dying right now. Kiowa stays with me for the rest of the night. I tell him to leave but he did not want to listen to me. A couple of hours later Taika shows up knocking on my room door. I am a crying mess and I don't want to see him right now. I was embarrassed at the way I look and I couldn't face his stares at me at that moment. Though he's my boyfriend things are not in a good place with us right now. Kiowa becomes pissed off as Taika walks in the room.

"Hey, Aquila, I heard what happened." He slowly walks into the room only seeing me from a distance.

"Don't come any further! I don't want you to see me right now." I remove the pillow from behind my head to cover my face.

There were just too many things going on around in my damn head I could not deal with everything. I start crying even more. Kiowa sees me in distress and forces Taika out of the room for me. Ki instantly went into protection mode. I'm not usually one of those girls who are an emotional mess, but in this one instance I think I must make an exception for myself. Taika didn't even put up a fight. As soon as he and Ki were on the opposite side of the threshold of my hospital room, the two of them stare each other down for about twelve seconds and then Taika walks away.

Ki comes back into the room by my bedside. "Aquila, you should get some rest. You really need it. And don't worry I will be here when you wake up. I promise you I'm not going anywhere, I'm here for you." He says leaning over my bedside.

I was in the hospital for three and a half weeks. Most of the time I was there I was alone. Of course Ki had to go to school and I didn't have much family that was available to come and see me. I used that time to focus on getting used to being alone. Kiowa would come to the hospital every day after school to give me company and brighten my spirit. He brought me my homework every day to help get my mind off things. I was in more pain about missing my parents than I was in physical pain. Having them gone made me feel like I had taken them for granted. I should have appreciated them more for all the things that had done for me. Today was the day I was checking out of the hospital and I was weary about going home to an empty house. Days I've longed for a quiet house while my parents were alive. But now I would give anything for the noise back. I would learn to tolerate the noise just to have my parents back.

Kiowa drives me home from the hospital. He is trying his hardest to make me feel better the best way he knows how to. There's this burning pain inside of me I must deal with. My life now is forever changed. I remember as a child that I used to say I couldn't wait to grow up. This is not what the fuck I meant at all. I am now forced to be an adult completely on my own even though I still had a few more months before I was out of high school. I could feel the depression settling in.

"Aquila, I just want you to know everything is going to be ok. You're not alone." Ki says as we drive to my house.

"I hope you are right. I need a little hope right now. Ki how am I going to deal with this? I'm all alone right now and I need someone to help me. I don't have a family anymore." I was just one big emotional wreck.

"Well let me be that someone who can help you through all of this. I'll be there only if you let me be there." He smiles. It did something for Ki to be my hero.

Once we reach my house it did not feel the same anymore. It was hard for me to even call this place my home. It was just a house I lived in, not a home but a house. I open the door and walk in to feel the eerie presence of nothing. Just air and the memory of what used to be of my parents. I make it up to my room and I sit on the edge of my bed. I take my mind off of missing my parents to realizing that it was no longer about them. I had to figure out how I was going to survive now. I want Kiowa to go home and let me be by myself. He didn't want to leave me but agrees to leave on one condition. The condition being that he can come back to check up on me in two hours. During this time I could see clearer than I could ever before at how much of a good heart Ki had. He was being an amazing friend to me.

I never realized how noisy the house could be until it was quiet. In this old house I could hear every squeak in the floor and all the settling noise. After Ki left I got up and walk around the house, exploring it like it was the first time that I had been in there. I was noticing things that I had never seen before and it was freaking me out. I cry a few times but eventually I had to pull myself back together. Ki came back to sit with me for the rest of the evening. It was good to have him there with me. I didn't think I would have survived the first night alone.

I return to school some two weeks or so later after leaving the hospital. Kiowa drives me to school the morning of my return. He did not have to do it but I was having anxiety about driving in a car. As I walk down the hallway I can feel everyone feeling sorry for me. It was all nice gestures, but I really could have done without people staring at me the entire time. It was like I was the new kid in elementary school that everyone was investigating. It was weird because people did not want to talk to me but they would surely stare out of curiosity. I want to avoid everyone because it was making me depressed. The stares only remind me of the horrid scars that were on my face. I want to run back home and get in my bed and cover my face. Being back at school that day made me realize that I haven't spoken to Taika since the day I asked him to leave when he came to the hospital. I saw him walking down the hallway toward me and instead of being happy to see him all I had was negative energy toward him. I only want people that was going to support me around me and not anyone that was going to make me feel bad – and Taika had a history of doing this with me.

"Hi, can we talk for a minute?" Taika says as soon as we're face-to-face. "Why wouldn't you allow me to come see you, but you let Kiowa come and see you? Why is he so damn special?" He says angrily. I couldn't believe that those were the first words to come out of his mouth. He was more concerned about how my accident affected him then how it affected me.

He pulls on my arm pulling me to the side of the school hallway. He had the nerve to be throwing a tantrum like a toddler. Although I had been in recovery for a month, I still had very sore areas on my body and the place where he grabs my arm was one of them. But he ignored my squirms and continues on his with his hissy fit. "Why wouldn't you let me see you? How come Kiowa got to see you and I didn't?" His says with flares in his nostrils.

"Taika, I wouldn't let you see me because I wanted to be alone! I don't want to deal with this right now." I start to walk away but I wasn't done yet. "And Kiowa was there because his mom told him were I was. She's my doctor you idiot." I yell.

"Ok, but I'm your boyfriend. And yet somehow he got to see you! I didn't! Do you know how that makes me feels?" He says frustrated.

"I'm sorry. Taika, I'm sorry." I didn't know what he wanted me to say and furthermore I couldn't believe he was being so selfish.

Talking to Taika and having a heated argument was not how I wanted to start off my first day back at school. He was the one being unreasonable but yet he had me feeling like I did something wrong. I force myself to shake him off and I move on throughout my day class after class. I was still uncomfortable about my scars, so in all my classes I choose to sit in the back of the class and hide so no one could see me. Even during lunch I sit at the lunch table alone purposely. Josh and Lilly attempt to keep me company but I got up and found another empty table to sit at alone. I couldn't understand why no one understood why I wanted to be alone.

I'm over in the corner trying to hide from everyone and I happen to overhear Taika with his friend. He didn't recognize it was me sitting alone because I had my head down with my hood on my head from my hoodie. I was stunned to realize he was talking about me. With my ears perked up but my head still down I tentatively listen to everything he and his friends were saying.

"Hey Taika, are you going to stay with her now that she's looks like she's been attacked by a bear? She looks disgusting." Alex, one of Taika, says while laughing.

"No, I was just with her because she was cute. Aquila used to be pretty. Now that she looks like that I'm done with her. As a matter of fact I never loved her anyway. Who can love someone who looks like that! I can't have anyone like that, but it was good while it lasted I guess." Taika had the biggest smile on his face.

I felt the blood boiling in my body. "Taika?! It's over you asshole!" I scream at him. I was my intention to finish listening to everything he was saying but I couldn't put myself through the torture of letting him make me feel lower than what I was already feeling.

I refused to baby sit his ego, how dare he make it out like he was a gift to me. It hurt to hear his vile words and I start crying and walk away from him – I feel like a coward for running away in the heat of the moment but I couldn't even look at him any longer. I went to my locker with a trail of tears following me. Kiowa sees me furiously packing my bag to go home. I was really upset and things only seem to get worse as the day progressed. It was like I had entered some type of parallel universe. I was emotionally stressed and mentally drained all in one day. No one understands what I'm dealing with right now. Instead of them trying to help they're only making things worse.

"Aquila, what's wrong? Why are you crying?" Kiowa says with worry.

"Taika's an asshole! I don't feel like being at school anymore. I'm going home. This is too much for me to handle right now." I could barely talk as the tears flow down my face and my voice was almost mute from the choking of pain in my throat. I didn't mean to just leave Ki standing there looking dumbfounded but I had to get out of there.

I left school a crying mess. I walk all the way home but it turns out to be a good idea because it helps me clear my mind. As I was walking suddenly something comes over me, an epiphany of some sort. I begin to realize that life is journey. You choose the road you walk, the people you meet, and how your life goes – well sort of. We may be able to change our looks and the way we act, but the one thing we can't change is our biology. We may be able to build skyscrapers and electronics to make our life easier, but we can't change what we were meant to do - which is to survive. We look at our situations and adapt by choosing the best survival method. And I made up my mind in that moment that I was going to survive by adapting.

After school Ki comes over to my house to find out what happened. I thought he was going to explode after I told him what Taika had said about me. He was so livid but I told him to let it go because I wasn't going to allow him to make me feel any worse than what I had already been feeling. I was in survival mode and I wasn't going to let anyone ruin that.

But it was hard being in survival mode because I was constantly fighting off the depression that was trying to take over my mind. I decide I need a little bit more time away from school so that I could get my mind together. Ki takes me over to his family's house every day to make sure I was not alone. He would not let me be depressed if he could help it. One particular day we decide to hang out at the beach for a little while, Ki says that he thought it would help me work through my thoughts and some fresh air always cheers people up. And he was right the beach was calm and relaxing. The birds were chirping and the sun was setting. It feels as if I was sitting in a movie scene. It was also the perfect setting for me to thank him for being so caring and to also ask him a question that had been on my mind.

"I have to thank you for caring so much about me throughout this situation. I just wanted to let you know I really appreciate it." I pause for a second and swallow hard as I work up the nerve to ask him the question. "Hey, I have a question for you. Why were you so pissed at Taika all the time?" I say shaking my head in confusion and wait for him to response.

"Aquila, I saw how unhappy you were with him. He has made you cry countless times in the last few weeks, and I could not sit quiet while that happened to you. You're an amazing girl and any guy would be lucky to have you on his side. Taika would rather have you wait for him than to push you forward. I couldn't help it but be very protective of you. Aquila, he does not deserve you like I deserve you. I mean we have been friends since we were in diapers, I cannot stand to see you hurt by him or anyone else. You complain about how you look. Aquila what you fail to realize is that you were beautiful before and you are even more beautiful after the accident. Whoever says you're not they don't understand beauty when they see it."

"Ki, my heart is still right now it does not even beat anymore. I don't know how to make it work again." I start crying. I look down at the sand burying my feet into it. Kiowa lifts my face up with his pointer finger and makes me look at him.

"Well let me make it beat for you. I'm not afraid of restarting your heart. I'm here, Aquila, I'm right here I am not going anywhere. I promise I will always be there for you no matter what." He smiles at me.

Hostile, but ever so sweet, I wonder if this will last forever. His lips so soft he kisses me with such passion. I can't believe this is happening. This is so wrong, but it feels so good. I have never felt this way before. This must be where I was meant to be. He was no longer my best friend. He existed in my life as my best friend, but re-entered as my companion. It might be the heavy pain killers causing me to move fast with him. Why not move fast for once? I have been living like a turtle for years. Dealing with the death of my parents became easier for me because of him. Life is becoming normal again and my heart starts beating again and stronger than ever before as I give in to the idea of Ki and I being us.

Things start to look up for me. You can say I became different in a way. I have never felt that way before. It was like I was a new and improved version of myself. Before I was like a shattered mirror and Kiowa put the pieces back together. Even when his hands start to bleed he still continues to fix the mirror. Being with Ki I begin to experience a different type of happiness.

Of course as our romance began to bud, Taika was sure to notice and with no surprise had huge issues with this arrangement. I notice that I would catch him watching me. I could be in the lunchroom and I could feel his eyes on me. I could be at my locker and Ki could have just left from meeting me and giving me a kiss. I would turn around and see him gazing at me. I feel like I'm a zebra and there's a lion stalking me trying to make me his dinner. It's starting to get weird and starting to scare me. How unnerving is it to turn around at any time and see someone staring at you? It's like he'd be undressing me with his eyes. It made my skin crawl and made me cautious stay away from him.

I honestly didn't think Ki and I dating would be such a big deal to anyone, but apparently everyone is shocked. But I guess I understand, everyone, including me, is so used to him just being my friend – and now he's my boyfriend. It's a big transition for me and everyone witnessing it. The whole school is talking about us and that's only adding more fuel to Taika's fire about us.

My Soul
(journal entry)

Although I've had some good days, every so often I slip into a dark place. Grief is funny like that. One day you can be fine and then the next out of nowhere sadness returns like it never left. There are no words to describe the pain that is in my heart. I have fallen into a dark place with no way out. I'm crying for an angel to come save me but there's no hope of that happening. I have lost all feeling as my body numbs and weakens by the day. I'm losing sight from the path that is in front of me. I'm starting to rust away like an old pickup truck in the summer time. I understand eventually everyone will have to die one day, but I'm so lost and confused right now I don't know. There's so much pain, loss, and depression that I'm dealing with I don't think I can handle any more of it. Somehow, I must pull myself out of this dark place to a place where I can be ok.

My soul has changed. There is a difference in me. I need an angel to save me. I was sitting outside in the dark looking up to the heavens above me. I was hoping for an answer of some sort. I feel alone but I wasn't, I needed some closure. I have not been to my parent's graves yet. At the time when they were buried I thought it would have been too much for me to deal with. But I think now it might be the best thing for me. This has been a completely emotional journey knowing that they are not here with me. Today I feel weak and brittle. There are things in this life we cannot change, and I understand that, but when it comes to being alone I cannot understand where to go from here – even with Ki on my side.

In the blink of an eye my mind has gone so far deep I feel like I'm writing my last words for my last day on this earth. I had a near death experience and now all I can see is death. My soul is so weak. Am I going crazy? It's hard to be able to build myself back up to the point of sanity. The bad days have returned and it's been hard for me to get the strength to get up out of bed.

I feel like I want to die and go and be with my parents. Honestly, I not sure if I have the will to live. As I contempt that thought I sit at this computer and write my last words. It sounds much easier than it actually is. I sit for hours trying to figure out what to write. There was nothing coming to my mind. Wow, such a significant thing to determine what you want the world to hear from you as your last words read at your funeral.

I was too injured to attend my parent's funeral. Ms. Maddox would have let me go, but being that I was still in a lot of pain I couldn't. If I make it out this funk I should probably go and see them. Poor Kiowa, he's trying his best to get me out of this funk. Unfortunately, the wound opened back up. My heart began to be still again. There is a fear holding me hostage and I don't know what to do.

I think about the word funeral. And something hits me and I can now write. From what I heard my parent's funeral it was sad – and that's understandable it was a tragic way to go out. And contrary to my parent's inability to get along they were loved by many. But what's crazy is when looking at the word funeral, the word fun jumps out at me. *Fun-eral.* I want to make the day I die fun. Yup, that's right, let's make it a joyous occasion. So here are my last words and testament. When you have a serious near death experience things aren't the same as they once were in the mind. You see all things pertaining to life in a different perspective. I know people may not want to laugh at my *fun-eral*, but one things for sure this would be one they'll never forget.

If you are reading this then that means that I died. There are a few things that I must say. I don't want anyone to be sad, but happy. I lived how many years. Yeah, cheer up it's OK. I have learned a lot in these few years. Some things are not forever and that includes life. I lived is the point I'm trying to make here. After all, there's another adventure that I must embark on. Even though I'm gone just know every time you think of me I'm here with you. I have loved being here, but I could not stay here anymore. I'm sorry I had to go. Hey, I lived, I loved, I cried, I loved life - well sometimes anyway. I will miss all who I have come across in my short time. From here on now I'm having fun. Whoever discovers this letter please read it at my funeral. I want everyone to know that I may be gone, but to remember that I have done everything that I wanted. After all I'm with God now, hopefully.

I don't want anyone to cry. At least you got to know me. I was a good friend, daughter, and a therapist to some. These are my last few words that you will hear from me for a while. I learned a lot. And I understood right from wrong. After all, I earned my wings. I maybe in the room and you may not know it. I wish I was the one helping you though this. I must tell you these wings feel so good! This place is so beautiful! Wow, wish you guys could be here. My soul is free. Freedom feels good! I will see some of you as the wind blows. Don't be sad, I told you I'm free! I want to thank all of you. There's something that all of you have done for me, and I will always remember for that. I want my funeral to be fun - after all it's in the word. Everyone should be dressed as they please.

Don't make my service long – take me directly to the gravesite. Let the pastor say a few words then throw me in the dirt. Then I want everyone to head over a park and have a party (if the weather permits – if not have it somewhere else) with music, good food, and jumping jacks for the kids. I want to put the fun back in funeral. I want my casket to be black, if possible, and I better not be in any crazy outfit or I will haunt you for the rest of your life. I want to be dressed in a nice black outfit. I want everything to be black. Tell you what, I have an even better idea just burn my ass up and be done with it. It's cheaper anyway than sticking me in the ground. I say all of this with love. I will always love you all.

Remember me for all the things that I did. I want everyone to know I love each and every last one of you all. Again, I must say, it is so amazing here. I wish you all could see it. Well bye for now. I will be with you always. I will miss you and I will always love you. I will see you in a blink of an eye.

Sincerely with love,

Aquila Waters

The letter I wrote was stupid, but I feel as though the point is made. I mean it would be kind of funny to have someone read the letter and I'm lying there dead in a casket. I'm starting to think these pain killers are starting to go to my head. The last couple of weeks I have been fascinated with death. It's almost like someone is writing a story about me – like someone is puppeteering my life through written words. You know like voodoo or something. I can tell you this thing, they're definitely making things worst for me. Maybe I guess that's how life goes, someone somewhere is writing a story about every last one of us. The author who is writing my story is doing a very nice job of screwing things up.

Reminiscing

I decided to go give the letter to Kiowa. Of course he had something to say about it. But I knew that I could count on Ki to do everything in his power to make sure that everything I put in that letter came true if I were to happen to die anytime soon. He says the letter was sad and he couldn't understand why I would write such a letter. He didn't understand that I was lost and was just trying to find my way out. I can't see the light at the end of the tunnel. Right now everything pitch-black in the tunnel, I'm trying to keep going but it feels like there is no end.

"Aquila, you're not going to die." He says in sad and strong tone. He seems almost agitated at the thought of me bringing this up.

"What if I get into another accident that can kill me? Or what if I fall off a cliff? Considering death has are many possibilities." I say nonchalantly.

"You won't die you're just traumatized because you lost your parents in the accident. Nothing is going to happen to you I promise. I love you and I'll protect you no matter what. Aquila,

I'm here for you if you need me. Right now, your world has changed so much I don't think you even know how much it has affected you. Trust me in time things will get better." He looks at me dead in my eye and for a split second I felt safe. But I quickly return back to reality. We are not here forever so why try to ignore the fact that one day we will not be here? I think if I see my parents' grave then I might be able to put my accident be hide me and move on with my life. While I had the courage I decide I was going to go this evening. I keep putting it off I might as well get it over with.

As the evening hits I pull myself together and walk the five miles to the grave yard. I take the time to clear my mind - praying to be strong enough to not have a break down in the cemetery. But I was unsuccessful at clearing my mind as I walk. The anxiety of seeing their names on the headstones or whatever they would have at their graves overtook me like nothing I've ever felt before. But I was halfway there now and it was no turning back.

I finally get to the cemetery gates. I stop for a second and take a deep breath and continue to walk up the brick road. The moment of truth has arrived and I walk up to the final resting place of Mika and Rhys Waters. I couldn't help but become overwhelmed with emotion. I start thinking of little moments with them. One stood out to me, I had completely worked both my parents' nerves because I wanted to have a sweet sixteen party. Now looking back on it I have no idea why I wanted a sweet sixteen in the first place. I have about six friends and I really didn't care that anyone else came to my party. I began to lay a guilt trip on myself and wondered how far I pushed them at times. Retrospectively, I realized that sometimes I got a kick out of challenging them. Usually I never want to do anything for my birthday. I remember even telling my mom one day to not even remember the day that I was born. But I don't know what came over me when I turned sixteen. I guess I wanted something I could look back on when I got old and grey and lived with sixty-four cats.

Anyway, back to the birthday thing. I think when I was turning sixteen I somehow convinced myself that this was the age that I finally would start to become my own person. I'm always so… well… awkward. Yeah, that's it, we can go with that. As I sit at the gravesite I realize my mom had raised me to be the person that I am. Come to think of it I'm a spitting image of her. She wanted me to be the opposite of her, but the thing is I can't. I look around at the teens today and, well, I'm the complete opposite. I think I was born in the wrong generation. I could not help but to laugh at myself. I fought my mom so much because she was fighting me and not allowing me to be who I was supposed to be. Yes, I'm only eighteen, but sometimes I feel like I'm eighty years old - just an old soul. I guess my mom could see that and wanted me to enjoy life. Why did she think I couldn't enjoy life just because I was an old soul?

As I sat and though more at the gravesite an eerie feeling came over me. I felt like someone was watching me visit my parents. I turned around but no one was there, but I did not feel comfortable. After all I'm alone in the dark in a cemetery. Doesn't it sound like a horror film to you? I started to make my way back down the brick road and head for home. I knew one thing about coming out here at night that I would never do it again. I have already been on the news once because of the tragic care accident, I didn't need to be on the news as murder victim.

Inside of Me

I feel completely different about seeing my parents, of course it was sad to see them like that, but it was good that I went to check on them. I still was a little frightened that feeling wouldn't leave me. I swear that someone was watching me the whole time I was out there. Kiowa's new thing now that we are in a relationship was that he likes to come over to my house every day to make sure I was ok. Also I know he was just being nosy as well. When I finally reached my house he was sitting on my pouch in a complete panic.

"Quil, where have you been?" He says hastily as he sees me coming up the sidewalk.

"At my parents' graves. What's wrong?" I say worried.

"Nothing, it's nothing." He calms down.

"No, something's wrong. Just tell me what it is!" I start to panic. I was already in a weird place from being at the grave yard and he didn't make it any better. My intuition was telling me something was wrong.

"It's nothing, Quil. I'm sorry I startled you. Let's go inside it's cold out here." He looks at me and tried to crack a smile.

Kiowa looked behind himself and out into the woods. It was almost like he was telling someone to back off. It was weird and very strange. Kiowa should know by now I can tell when he's lying. There's something he's not telling me and I'm determined to figure it out. Ki ended up staying the night. He says it was too late for him to go home and he asks to sleep on the couch. Kiowa's very old school and like to treat girls with respect. He claims it's his way of not being like his father, whatever that means - I thought I was the only one with daddy issues.

Although Ki was in the next room he got me to thinking about family. I saw qualities in him that were completely opposite of my dad. Just like Ki and his daddy issues, I had some of my own. After seeing the way my dad was with my mom, I knew that wanted a husband who was not going to neglect his family. A man who wouldn't just leave his wife at home to raise his daughter alone while he stayed out all night with his friends. I didn't want a man that if we had children, especially a daughter, that he would neglect her all her life and then once the daughter gets a boyfriend decides to start caring about her. My dad did that to me, and I'm sorry, but it was too little, too late for him and I to try to have some type of relationship after all the years of neglect. A part of me misses him and the other part of me doesn't, but every single atom that was used to form me misses my mom.

My mom was, and still, is my world. I never knew how important she was until she died. I miss her every day. So much so, that it turns my stomach into a knot. That's when I realize how much I loved her. I can never get that type of love again. That type of love is only given once. Then one day you wake up and it's gone. I never thought that at this young age I would have had to bury my mom. There is so much that I still need to learn from her. I don't know what I'm going to do when I'm pregnant and need someone to help me understand what motherhood is all about. I guess I'm on my own now and must solve everything by myself with no help. That's the story that's written for me.

Falling Rain

I finally return back to school after much convincing from Ki and Ms. Maddox. The thought of attending summer school to make up for the lost time was enough convincing for me to get me stuff together. But school is so boring as of late. I cannot wait to graduate! Only a couple of more months is what I keep telling myself. Going to school now was so daunting. Not that I loved it so much before, but the accident has changed the experience for me so much. All anyone ever does is staring at me. Like, hello? What's the big problem? Why are you looking at me? Is what I want to say every time I catch someone staring at me. I get, it I'm scary looking, but stop staring at me!

I was in such a rush to get to AP English today that I ended up bumping into Taika. I have not spoken to him since we broke up. Ki was in my life and now and I was happy. I no longer needed to put up with Taika's bullshit.

"I'm sorry." Taika says quickly before I had a chance to run away from him.

"Yeah it's whatever." He was somewhat in my path so I tried to get around him.

"So... how have you been?" He says smiling as he steps in my path when I move to the left to get around him.

Clearly he wasn't going to let me get away so I engaged in the conversation. "Ugh...good I guess." Since things were already uncomfortable I decided to ask the hard question. "So, why are you always staring at me in class?" I ask folding my arms.

He smiles. I think he thought he was getting a breakthrough. "Because I miss you!" He smiles again assuming I was going to be happy that he missed me.

"I'm not going through this again. I'm with Kiowa now and you know it. This thing between us, this game you're playing, has to stop." I push passed him and start to walk away.

"He can't always protect you. Just like when you were out there in the cemetery late last night." He says and his voice follows me as I walk away.

It stops me dead in my tracks. "Wait, how you know I was..." I take a pause and an unnerving feeling flushes over me. I roll my eyes at him and walk away as quickly I could. This was getting weird, scary weird and I didn't want any parts of it. Taika messed up my mind, I could not even pay attention in AP English. All I could think about was him stalking me. His creepy ass is always watching me, who knows what he's plotting in that head of his. If he's going to be a problem I need to deal with him now, but how is the question.

I was contemplating not going to my next class because Taika and I were in that class together. I decided to be brave and just bare it – it's not much he can do to me in a classroom full of people. He watches me the entire class and I could tell he was just trying to get in my head. When class was over I darted out of there as if my life depending upon it. I was walking down the brick, crowded hallway just trying to get to my locker. Suddenly Kiowa comes up behind me and I scream. I was already on edge so scares the living hell out of me. Everyone stop for a second and looks at us and then go back to their business. I laugh it off but I was really thinking it was Taika with a knife at my neck trying to kill me. Taika was like a ghost because as I turn around to hug Ki my eyes lock with Taika just standing to the corner looking at us. I cringe in the inside.

"Hey, beautiful. I'm sorry. I did not mean to scare you." Ki says smiling. He kisses me and hands me a dozen of cobalt blue roses. I have never in my life seen blue roses. They were so pretty and smelled like normal damn roses, but were to die for. It takes my mind off Taika's crazy ass.

"Thank you. These are so beautiful. How did you get them to be so blue?" I smell the roses to take in their scent again.

"Well, that's a secret. I know your favorite color is cobalt blue so, yeah, I made it happen. This is my way of asking my girlfriend out on a date Saturday." He laughs.

"Ok what time Saturday? Are you coming to pick me up?" I smile and laugh.

"Whenever you're ready, my love. I know beauty takes time, and trust me, beautiful is what you are." Kiowa says charmingly.

I suddenly forget all my problems and worries with Taika. Kiowa seems to take all that worry and stress away. I can't help getting lost in those chocolate brown eyes and his straight long

black hair complementing his tan skin. Ki also has a chiseled

jawline, not to mention dimples, teeth as white as snow, and a

smile that will make you melt. I came back to reality when I

realized that I had physics class next. I get knots in my stomach but

I quickly get my act together. I don't want to say anything to Ki

because I know he'll try to play hero.

I get to class and search for Lilly, my best friend. She's

nowhere to be found and then I suddenly remember that she went

on vacation with her family. Like, who takes their children on

vacation in the middle of a school semester? Our teacher Mrs.

White, or Mrs. Hates as us students like to call her, decides today

she wants us to working partners today. Your best friend is

supposed to be there for you during crucial moments like these. If

you want to know why I'm tripping it's because Taika sits right

behind me. And it's just my luck his partner happens to be out of

school today too, so guess who I get stuck with? My psycho ex

who can't seem to leave me alone.

Taika thought everything was all good. He comes over to

sit by me in his charm, but I wasn't having that. Because I had to go back and have a minor surgery on my face I had stitches in. I attempted to play like my face was in pain so I can be excused out of the office to go to the nurse's office for some pain pills. But Mrs. White must have been on her period because she was acting like a bitch and would not let me go and sent me right back to my seat. The only hope I had was a hurricane to happen out of nowhere, but unfortunately, I was not that lucky.

"Aquila…" I cut Taika off right there before he could even finish his statement.

"No, I don't want to talk to you. The only thing I want to do is work on this experiment." I was so pissed that I got stuck with him.

"Ok, you know I only saw you because my dad is buried out there. I know what I said earlier sounded creepy. It's not safe for your to be out there alone by yourself. You still are a girl." He just looks at me.

I really didn't believe him. If that's the case why didn't he just say that in the first place, but whatever maybe it was true. His delivery of it sucked though.

"Could you hand me the copper powder?" I choose to ignore him.

"Wow, you're really not listening to me?" He looks confused.

"I told you the experiment is all I'm worried about. Taika, you had your chance and you blew it. I don't know how many times I ask you to clean up your attitude with me? It's over just let it die." I look over at the clock to see how much time we had left – too much time.

"You know I loved you." He says.

I roll my eyes at him and look at him very stupidly – this is where I snap. How can you be so rude to the one you love? Did he really believe what he was saying? He never loved me, and I know he didn't because now I see what love is supposed to be and feel like.

"You love me? Ha! Yeah, right. Then why did you say those entire horrible things about me?" I look at the clock again to see if any more time had passed.

"Sorry…" He tried to continue his sentence but I cut him off.

"Don't you dare try to interrupt me? You had your chance. Don't get mad when you see someone else treating me better than you ever did!"

"So, we are really over? No more you and me just you and Kiowa? These four months meant nothing?" His tone was sad but it didn't have any effect on me.

"Yes, me and Ki are on for now. High school love is not meant to last anyways." I smile sarcastically. I looked at him with utter disgust, and all we did was work on the experiment for the rest of the class time. After a while the bell finally rings. After his class, Ki must have run from his other class because he was right outside the door waiting for me.

"What's wrong you look so pissed?" He asks concerned as he sees the look on my face.

"Nothing it's just Taika…" Ki cuts me off.

"Taika! What the hell did he have to say to you?" He says soon joining the pissed off party.

"Nothing, I think he gets the point now." I say smiling.

"The point?" Ki says in a puzzling tone.

"That I love you and not him. He had his chance. Now it's time for me to have someone in my life that truly loves me." I kiss him and give Ki a hug. He smiles at me and I knew that it was just me and him from now on.

The Unknown

I feel that I was back in a good space again. And I pray, hopefully once and for all, that I have Taika off my back. I was able to get my happiness back and think I may have finally come into a place of acceptance about my parents' deaths. Kiowa picks me for school this morning which is our normal routine now. He also brought me breakfast which was good because it was so early that I did not get a chance to eat. When we arrive at school we agree that we would meet in the lunchroom. I needed to put my things away and Ki needed to grab is paper from one of his classes. When I get to my locker to get my textbook a letter falls out. I pick it up off the dusty floor. The envelope did not have a name on it. I assumed it to be another sorry for your loss letter – even after all this time I'm still getting letter like that. When I opened it, I was so shocked to see what it was. I could have had a heart attack. It was an apology letter from Taika. I don't know how to feel about all of this. He was still trying to win me over. But I really did not have any time for his shit, so I just stuffed the letter into the bottom of my bag and went on with my day.

I can't say that I wasn't curious about what he wrote in the letter. When I got home after school and was sitting on the floor doing my homework I got distracted with the thought that the letter was in my book bag. I really did not give a crap about doing my homework, but I was in the home stretch of graduation so I knew I needed to finish and just get it over with.

I was distracted again and was looking for my blue flower pen that my mom has given me. I peeked in my bag but I didn't see it right away. There was so much crap in my book bag that I just decide to dump the entire contents of my bag on the floor. Well, well, what have you? The damn pen somehow attached itself to Taika's letter. It was evident that I should read the letter, so I just decide to give in a read it.

Aquila, I'm sorry about all that I have put you through these last couple of weeks. This is my apology to you. I have been a complete jackass to you. I see you with Kiowa and I now realize your worth. I miss you and I should have treated you better. I wanted to get in touch with you so that I can officially apologize for the way I have acted as off lately. I know that I have acted like a horrible boyfriend.

I have fabricated a lot of lies and have treated you horribly. I can't forgive myself knowing that I have let you get away from me. Hopefully this will make everything right with you. I'm so sorry. Please forgive me. I'm not lying to you anymore. I know that your heart belongs to Kiowa. He makes you smile and laugh. I hope you're doing better. You're my one who got away.

~Taika

Wow, he seems really broken without me in his life. But he had his chance with me. He had more than one chance and he blew them all. We weren't together that long, he shouldn't be that bothered by it. Hopefully this situation between us is over. Now it's time for someone else to appreciate me.

Saturday Night

It was Saturday night and date night for Kiowa and me. I have never spent the entire day getting ready before, but for Kiowa I did. I was nervous for some reason I didn't understand why. He drives us to the beach, the day was calm and peaceful. The beach is empty only he and I would be occupying the sand. As we were walking he picks me up and decides to carry me to the beach – it made me smile but I told him he didn't have to but he insisted. Kiowa says angels should not have to walk – how flattering. He had candles lighting the path and once we get to the end of the path there was a white blanket with blue roses on it.

"Aquila, I need to tell you something that has been on my mind lately." Kiowa says smiling

"Sure, what is it?" I ask nervously.

"I need you in my life to make me a better man. I see us one day getting married and starting a family together. I don't want to ever treat you horribly. I want to treat you like the queen you are. I want you to know how deeply I'm in love with you this is where my heart belongs."

I blush. "Kiowa that's the sweetest thing I have ever heard." I smile like there was no tomorrow.

We spent two hours on the beach cuddling. We stay to watch the sunset – it was one of the most romantic days I've ever had. Kiowa drives me back home. As I was getting ready to get out the car I can't resist from kissing him good night. The passion was so intense that we started making out. I get out of the car and ask Kiowa to come into the house. I was a bit nervous but I was ready for this to happen. He's the person I'm comfortable with giving myself, all of myself, to.

We walked up the staircase into my bedroom. Kiowa lays me on the bed. He climbs on top of me and unzips my dress exposing my black lace bra. I ripped open his white button-down shirt. He kisses my neck and goes lower and lower. Things escalated even more and we ended up having sex right then and there. After we had sex we just lay staring into each other's eyes. The next morning Kiowa make me breakfast and we were sitting in the kitchen just gazing at each other.

"How are you, Quil?" He asks with a smile.

"Little sore, thanks." I smile and laugh a little. I think I was slightly embarrassed.

"Quil, I love you. You know that?" He smiles grabbing my hand.

"Yes, I know that." I smile back. We were both so giddy.

"Well, I have to leave to go to work. I'll come by after I get off. You're the best thing that has ever happened to me. I can't imagine my life without you. I love you." He says not wanting to leave and then he leans down to kiss me on the forehead.

"Ok, I love you too." I say as I watch him walk away.

I went back up to my room to change the sheets off the bed. There was blood on them from my hymen breaking. After the sheets were washed I put them back on the bed and I jumped in the shower. I thought to myself that Kiowa has truly changed me in a good way. Which made me smile from ear to ear uncontrollably.

Beautiful Clouds Arising

In the weeks after me and Kiowa had sex I felt a little weird in my body. It was like I did not even know who I was anymore. I think Kiowa is changing me for the better, he's bringing out a side of me that I haven't seen before. I was not worried about my parents anymore. I'm damn sure not worried about Taika anymore. Things in my life, for once, seem OK. I'm at peace with my parent's death and I'm at peace with the way my face looks. I feel like a new and improved me. Kiowa and I have been inseparable. I'm completely and utterly head over heels in love with him. I'm so close to graduation that I can hardly wait. I'm so over school. I want to begin my life and be considered an adult. I want things to be the same way before my parents had died and before the fighting.

It was Monday night Kiowa invited me over to a dinner/council meeting with his family. I was kind of skeptical to go because this means Taika would be there, but I went anyway. Much time has passes and I'm over him and it appears he may have moved on as well. When I arrive I found out Taika wasn't going to be there anyway. So that definitely ensured for a peaceful night. There was a beautiful full moon out that night. Kiowa mom's house was close to a cliff, the house was perfectly set in a way that it feels like we could literally touch the moon. Its beauty was radiant that night as the moon was so big. I had never seen the moon so close. I got up to go get a closer look and Kiowa came up behind me and wrapped his arms around me. I place my hands on top of his. It's like a scene out of a movie - a perfect night, a perfect couple. He kisses me on my neck which makes me shiver a little.

"Hey, beautiful, what are you thinking about?" He asks confidently.

"Nothing, what about you?" I say wondering.

"Well since you ask, I'm imaging how beautiful you will look in a long white gown. The feeling I'm going to have seeing you walk down the aisle to me. The beauty of our first kiss as husband and wife. Also, how I'm going to spend the rest of my life with the woman who has my heart." He says with such detail.

I turned around to look at him in his eyes. He's wearing a white dress shirt that was unbuttoned most at the top with black pants. While I was wearing a coral dress that was loose and flowing when the wind blew. My hair was tied back into a ponytail.

"Ki…" He cuts me off.

"Let me talk, ok. Aquila, I love you so much that I'm afraid of losing you. I can't imagine my world without you. I don't see myself being with anyone else other than you. Every time I consider your eyes it's like looking God in the eyes. I thank him for bringing you into my life. I don't know what I would do without you." He gets down on his knee.

I can see everyone watching us out the corner of my eye. His Mom stood out the most because she had been setting the table up. She had a set of plates in her hand and she dropped them when he got on his knee and ran to get her camera. She made sure she would not miss a minute of it.

"Aquila Grace Waters, will you do me the honor of becoming my wife and make the rest of my days like having heaven on earth? It will be an honor to have you as my wife. Quil, will you marry me?" He says with tears rolling down his face.

I start to cry. Everything he says was so poetic and beautiful. I knew Kiowa loved me, but what I did not know was how deep that love went. I wiped the tears from his eyes.

"Kiowa, yes! You make me happy every single day. Everything that you have done for me makes me feel superhuman. I can't see my days without you anymore." He gets up off his knee and puts the ring on my finger.

We start to walk back towards everyone – we're both smiling and glowing from what just happened. Ms. Maddox looks like she's about to explode she was so happy. I honestly had never seen her that happy before. She hugs me so tightly I thought that I was going to suffocate.

"I already consider you my daughter, Aquila. Now it will be official! My son, I'm so very proud of you! I can't believe you surprised us all with this. Oh, I'm so happy for the both of you! This is the best news that I have ever heard all week!" She says with such passion.

Once the excitement of our engagement died down a bit the meeting of the two tribes went on. This meeting was very important. It is designed to keep the peace between the Catori

Tribe and Nita. Kiowa and I are a part of the Catori, or spirit tribe, and Taika was a part of the Nita, or better known as the bear tribe. A long time ago there was a battle between both tribes over land which resulted in them hating each other. After the huge blood bath both chefs decided to come up with a treaty and every two months there is a dinner between our tribes with the Council of Elders.

I could not even pay attention to everything that was going on. I was too busy thinking about what just happened and that I was engaged. I can't believe that I'm in love with my best friend. Kiowa kept staring and grinning at me. Suddenly he grabs my hand and guides me to the car.

"The night is not over with us, Quil." He says with a strong tone.

"Oh, it's not." We begin to smile at each other.

"No, it's not." He smiles again.

The drive was not that long, Kiowa ends up taking me to the beach – this was becoming our spot. He pulls the car into the parking lot and got out and opens my car door. I was not prepared to go for a stroll on the beach, hell, I was not prepared to be engaged tonight, either.

"Kiowa, I'm kind of unprepared for the beach." I say softly and innocently.

"Well, I was planning on carrying you in the first place."

"Oh. Uh… Ok." I was unsure what all he was doing.

Kiowa picks me up. I was more attracted to him then I had ever been since knowing him. I was so amazed at him.

"You're really strong, Ki." I blush as I was saying it.

"You didn't realize that when we had sex I wanted to do something special for you." We chuckle.

He planned for us to dance under the stars that night. There was classical music playing in the background and the atmosphere was romantic. I felt that I could fly and Kiowa was up there with me. Before my accident I had never seen this side of Kiowa it's like he's a completely different person to me. We dance under the stars all night long then we watched the sun come up. I have never felt this type of emotion for one person in my entire life. I guess I feel asleep on the beach because I woke up in my room with Kiowa next to me. When I woke up Kiowa had his arms wrapped around me like he's protecting me. I can only think and say to myself, wow this must be a dream.

Kiowa explained to me that the ring he gave me was his grandmother's ring. When his grandmother died his grandfather gave him their rings. He told Kiowa to only give his grandmother's ring to the one he truly could not live without. He promises his grandfather that he wouldn't give it to anyone he didn't love, I guess that person is me.

"Kiowa, I love you so much!" I couldn't help but say as I put my arm on top of this arm that was holding me and squeeze him tightly.

"I love you, too." He replies back.

When Monday morning came around I could not be happier. My weekend was great, I was engaged and it was officially that last day of school. I am elated to finally becoming an official high school graduate. Because we got engaged at the meeting of the tribes everyone already knew about our engagement. The entire school was talking about it. When I ran into Lilly she immediately runs over to me and hugs me.

Our last day went on smoothly and calmly. The next thing I had to worry about was prom, which personally I didn't feel like going. It was custom for our school to have prom the week before we graduated. I wasn't impressed with prom because planning my wedding was more on my mind. I thought prom would be a waste of money and time when I can be doing something better. Also I was thinking that after I graduate was going to continue to run my mom's store. I could have actually sold the store, my parents left me enough insurance money that I didn't have to worry about money for a while. But I needed to do something and get busy. I decide that I would talk to Ki about it later when we were together.

Later, that day Kiowa drove me to his Mom's house. We lay on the ground outside. I turn toward him and placed my head on his chest. I start dreaming about our future with each other.

"Kiowa, what's our next move going to be now that we're done with school? I can't just consider me anymore. I have to think about you since we are getting married." I say snugly deeper into his chest.

"It should go something like this - prom, graduation, wedding, and spending the rest of my days with you. In a couple years we will try for a baby." Kiowa just laughs at me.

"You know I have never believed in fairytales until now. Just to let you know you're going to be lucky to get one kid out of me. Don't think you're going to be popping one hundred kids out of me." We both laugh at the thought of so many kids. I change my mind about bringing up opening back the store, Ki didn't seem like h was ready for that conversation.

Kiowa's mom was still in the clouds about us being engaged. She went on and on about what everything should look like. I don't like too much attention to be on me, but I guess I will have to deal with it.

"Quil, we have to go dress shopping for your prom!" She exclaims.

"Ugh, I guess I have to go right. Can't I just miss it?" I say nervously.

"No, you cannot. I'm not going to allow you to miss a night of excitement. This is the last big high school event. Plus it's practice for the wedding. Why do you not want to go?" Ms. Maddox and Ki both want to know the answer to that question.

"I'm still a little insecure about my face. I don't really want to have a lot of people looking at the girl whose face is chopped like a piece of wood put through a chopper." I say with a stern voice.

"Quil, no one else matters but me and you. I think you're the most beautiful thing that I have ever had graced my presence. I don't know why you can't see that." He says with a sweet tone.

"Yeah, I know that but I still don't like the way I look. It's a girl thing you wouldn't really understand." I say looking down at the ground playing in my hair.

I still will forever question how I look no matter what Kiowa tells me. Everyone around me must realize that I must come to terms with everything that has happened to me. No one else can understand how I feel. I'm the one who makes decision about my life. I guess that must change since I'm now engaged. It still feels weird to say that I'm going to get married. I never thought that I would walk down the aisle. But one thing my parent's marriage taught me is that I refuse to be a lonely housewife. I'm going to keep my identity and I will make the most of my marriage.

Kiowa is starting to change me in ways that I have never experienced before in my life. I feel that things are going a bit too well for us. It's like someone's sitting at a computer and writing this story. If I know my life and through everything that has happened to me. This fantasy will not last too long – I don't mean to be negative but I don't want anything catching me off guard.

I decide to take Kiowa's advice. It's one night of my life I can spare a few hours out of my life to go shopping. Ms. Maddox took me to a dress shop in town. I tried on what seemed like hundreds of dresses. My feet were hurting so badly by the end of the day, but I happy to have found one strapless dress that I like. Of course, it was a cobalt blue. Kiowa's Mom was so happy I think she enjoyed it more than I did.

Two days later it was prom night, the biggest night for a high school student. I got all dressed up. My hair was done and makeup and I was waiting on Kiowa to get ready, which it should have been the other way around. Ms. Maddox wants me to do a grand entrance to show everyone. She says that it was practice for the wedding – everything was practice for the wedding according to her. I walk down the creaky, noisy wooden stairs down to everyone. Kiowa and I made eye contact as soon as I get to the bottom of the stairs.

"You look absolutely beautiful!" He says smiling from ear to ear.

"Thanks, you look great yourself." I say nervously, but I'm smiling and feel good.

After Ms. Maddox took a million pictures of us we get in the car and drive to the banquet hall. Everyone was looking amazing, I, however, never felt more out of place. However, I shake off the insecurity and join in the festivity with everyone else. We danced all night, but then I begin to get that feeling again that someone was watching me. I sense that Taika was nearby, but I didn't care.

Suddenly the music was interrupted and our principal came on stage to announce the prom king and queen. This honestly always goes to the two most beautiful people in the school. It never goes to the two most hard-working students in the school.

"I hope you all are having a good time tonight. It's now the time that you all have been waiting for." Everyone is standing around in anticipation waiting to hear who will be crowned as king and queen. "The Class of 2016, prom king and queen is Kiowa and Aquila. Come to the center of the room for the spotlight dance." He says enthusiastically.

I was frozen. I did not expect for us to be named the king and queen. "Ki, I don't want to do this. This is not right." I say with much anxiety.

"Come on. I will be right there with you. I'm not going to leave you." He says reassuring me.

"We can just leave no one would notice. You know I don't like dancing." He pulls me by my hand guiding me to the front. He forces me to face my insecurity.

My heart was beating so quickly I thought that my heart was going to come out of my chest. I was completely out of my comfort zone. They crowned us and I just felt that I was going to pass out. Kiowa must have saw how nervous I looked because he wanted to make sure I was ok.

"Quil, I love you and I'm so happy to be with you." He says as he's pulling me close and we're slow dancing.

Still looking around at everyone looking at us, I whisper to Ki. "I love you, too, but please get me the hell out of here."

"Yeah, no. You're going to stand here and dance with me. Besides the dance is almost over." He says calming me down. I can tell he thought I was over reacting.

To my relief that song ends and we were no longer the center of attention. Kiowa asks me if I was ready to go home and of course I say yes. We sneak out and he drives me home. I was so tired I pass out in the car when I wake up I was in Kiowa's bed – can't remember anything else from the night

The week has pass after prom night to end the senior year. I'm the valedictorian the top of my freaking class – even after all the time I missed due to the accident I still managed to make the top of class. I had to come up with a speech to give to the graduating class and it was proving to be hard to do. I try staying up to write it but I eventually pass out with pen in hand and paper under my hand. I was trying all morning to think about what I was going to say at graduation day. Kiowa's mom tried to give me motherly advice, but I was too busy trying to fake a heart attack so I would not have to go. The drive to the graduation was very short and I still had nothing to say. We get out the car and walk up the cobblestone road into the school gym.

Staring at the graduation program I became nervous seeing my name listed – where was all this anxiety coming from I ask myself. Since I was at the top of my class I was sitting on stage next to all the teachers. I told Kiowa before going up to the stage that he might want to catch me when I pass out. As I sit on the stage I catch Ki's eye and he gives me a reassuring look and mouths to me to relax. The principal walks up to the podium and introduces me. As I attempt to get up I can feel my leg wobble like noodles. I couldn't understand why I was so nervous. Kiowa and his family were cheering me on trying to give me some encouragement.

I walk up to the podium and initially stumble over my words. "I uh… I don't have a speech prepared. I could not think of anything to say. The only thing I did was come to school and try to survive. All of us have gone through changes. No one in here has gone through a change like I did. Most of you may know me from the news. My parents died in a terrible accident. My mom gave her life for me to be able to live. I don't know how to thank her for that. If my parents were here they would be the annoying parents in the audience with a bullhorn shouting my name and constantly interrupting. I guess what I'm trying to say is, I made it through high school not in one piece but I made it - we made it. If you think about it I should be dead, but I'm not. I'm here to take on the world like everyone else. I hope we all can keep in touch. To my fiancé, Kiowa Maddox, I look forward to walking down the aisle and becoming your wife. To Ms. Maddox you have been there with me through it all, along with Kiowa to help pick me up. I can never replace my mom, but you are my second mom. There are two people that couldn't make it here to see me give this speech and to see me walk across the stage – but I know they're watching me from somewhere. Thank you and have a great night." I tried to get through my speech calmly.

I step down from the podium and I receive a standing ovation. I turned around and smile. I was not expecting it but I was grateful. The graduation process continues on as the principle calls all the graduation students' names one by one. Once everyone's name was called we're all dismissed and are now official high school graduates. I could not be happier to be out of school. This year has been the most exhausting. Now I'm ready to get home and relax and enjoy the graduation festivities.

As I sit at the graduation party I begin to think about what was next for Kiowa and I. There's a part of me that thinks we are moving a little too fast, but I think that's natural as we're making a huge move. We literally just graduated high school and soon I'll be a wife. I think for right now I just want to hold off on any wedding. Things are starting to look like a clear picture again. In both of our lives people who have gotten married marriages didn't last long and that scares me. I was already having anxiety and on top of that everyone wanted to talk about our upcoming wedding and our engagement – I rather not. I escape from the conversations and find my way to the food table to get something to eat. Out the corner of my eye I see Ayana, Taika's sister, walking towards me. She hasn't been talking to me lately, which I'm ok with seeing how I ended things with Taika. I can't blame her for being on her

brother's side. I stopped looking at the food the closer she gets.

"Hey, Aquila, how are things going?" She says in a weird

tone.

"Things are going good." I say with a soft polite voice.

"So, what's your plan now that we are done with high

school? College?" She asks.

"I'm going to hold off from school for right now. I'm going

to finally open my mom's store again. How about you? What's

your game plan?" I say with a smile on my face.

"I'm going to get a job for right now. I think I need time off

from life right now. There are some things I have to work out right

now. I haven't decided on school yet." She says nervously.

"Are you ok?" I say concerned.

"Yeah, but Taika isn't. He's heartbroken, Aquila!" It was

almost like she couldn't wait to get that off her chest. "Don't you

get it? You broke his heart? He's in pain. All he thinks about is

you. He wanted to be there for you after the accident but you

pushed him away. Now it's all about Kiowa! Funny how you

jumped from my bother over to Kiowa so easily without giving Taika a chance." She says angrily.

Wow, I didn't see that coming from her at all. "Taika and I were on the rocks before the accident. I get it, me and Ki are moving fast but we are not getting married anytime soon. I'm woman enough to admit to my wrongs. I do owe him an apology for how things ended between us. We were doomed from the start, though. You don't know everything we went through and your brother is completely innocent." I say with a stern voice.

"Aquila, just know that you weren't the only one who was hurt when your parents died. I don't think it was just your parents who died, a part of you did as well." She storms off.

She walked away from me to go hang out with some of her friends. I thought to myself about what she says. I do agree that I ended things on a bad note when I and Taika broke up. If he was going through something he should have reacted in a more mature way. But I'm no longer concerned about my ex, I'm looking forward to my future. I'll take the blame for a lot of things but my relationship with Taika, I'm not.

I walk over to Kiowa and ask him for the keys to my car. He stands there for a second and starts smiling at me. I look into his eyes and start smiling. There's just something about him that make the world stop and my heart beat faster than what it should. I don't know what it is, I try and tell myself heart be still but it won't when I'm around Ki. He reaches in his pocket and hands me the keys.

"Now, where do you think you're going?" Jared, Ki's friend, says and laughs.

"Come on, Aquila stay for a while. It's not like we have school in the morning." Joe, another friend, says. He was smiling too.

"No, we don't have school, but I need to reopen my mom's store in the morning. So, I need to get some rest." When I says that Kiowa looks at me with this weird expression on his face. I look at him with a smile and give him a not now look.

"Aquila, are you sure you're ready to open the store again? Maybe this is too soon?" Casey says with concern.

"I think I am. Otherwise, what's the point of holding on to it? I ordered new snacks and knick-knacks a couple of weeks ago.

There being delivered tomorrow. So yeah I think I'm ready." I say taking a deep breath.

"Alright now, leave my beautiful fiancé alone. If she says she's tired, she's tired, come on I'll take you home." Kiowa says. We walk out the party together.

"Aww, Kiowa you have gone soft on us." They all say and laugh.

"Soon we are not going to hear from you." Joe says sarcastically.

"Yeah, Kiowa will be too busy with being married to come hang with us." Jared says.

"Now you guys have nothing to worry about. You guys will still be able to hang out." I yell back to the guys laughing as we're leaving.

"Guys, even if that does happen that's perfectly fine with me I have the most perfect women on my side. I'm building a life with her." Ki yells as he unbothered by their taunts.

We walk to the car and drives to my house. During the entire ride I look out the window. Kiowa starts tickling me, he can tell I'm deep in thought and tries to break my concentration. I tell him to watch the rode. He wants to talk I had this gut feeling, but I really wasn't ready to. I turn on the radio to avoid the talk. But soon we get to the house and now we're in awkward silence as he turns the car off and we get out.

"Kiowa, I know you want to talk about something I can feel it." I say as I decide to just get things over with.

"It nothing. I just…you know, now that we are going to be getting married why didn't you tell me that you were going to open the store again?" He asks curiously.

"I just thought it was time, you know? I think that I have grieved enough and since we aren't in school anymore I need something to do. It's just time. I debated selling it for a while and working somewhere else. It just didn't seem right giving it away. I wanted to talk to you about it but I just never found the right time." I say reassuring him.

"Quil, I support whatever you want to do you know that. You could have talked to me. But I wanted to talk about the wedding." He says.

"Oh… Well, actually I've been thinking about that as well. I think we should give it a year, at least. We need time to settle into our new lives. I love you just know that nothing is going to change that. I just want you to know that." Smiling from ear to ear hoping my charm would get him to see things my way.

"I agree with that. We're on the same page. I thought you were going to be sad about it. I know one day you will be my wife I'm perfectly fine with waiting." We smile at each and I open the door to get out the car.

Sturdy Oak

Since my mom is gone I'm finding that life is like a glass house. Throw a rock and that shit comes crashing down and there is several thousand pieces of glass all over the place. I have heard that there's no way to fix a broken piece of glass. To permanently repair it you have to reheat the glass to 1700°C (3090°F) and let it melt and make a whole new glass house. To remake the glass house, it will take months maybe even a couple years but it is possible to make a glass house new again.

It was time for me to repair the broken glass house of my mom's store. It's been almost a year that the store has been closed and I really didn't know what I was walking into going into the store. I take the car and drive to the corner of Rosemont and Canal where the store is located. The drive is only and about half an hour, but it felt like a never-ending drive. I hadn't been to the store since the accident. I'm choosing to take back my life with the help of Kiowa and his family I can breathe again.

As I got closer to the store my heart and my brain were fighting each other. Eventually I arrived to the store and I had to be brave. Even though I have seen this same building thousands of times it looks completely different. I slowly start to get out the car making my way to the door. The bushes had grown over a lot and needed to be trimmed down. They'd grown so much they covered all the windows of the store. The rose bush that was once planted in front of the store died because no one tended to it – and it's hard to kill a rose bush. They were so dry you could use them to start a fire. The place looked abandoned, which it was, if you think about it. After the accident things just died off. The store looks like how I fell in the moment – like death.

It seemed like a long walk to the door of the store. There were so many memories that happened here it was hard to forget. There was the time I was riding my scooter and fell flat on my face. My mom stopped helping with a customer she rushed over to hug me. There was also that time when I, Lilly, and Kiowa were running in the street, we were seconds away from being hit by a car. My mom was pissed at us for playing in the street. Funny how I keep almost dying by cars. I should have been dead a long time ago. Maybe I'm just destiny to die in a car accident. If at this point in my life I can make a deal with God I would. At some point, I

seem to be very good at cheating death. I have had too many

people risk their lives to save mine.

I gazed at the door before unlocking the store, I stopped.

My feelings start to coming over me. I put my feelings aside last

night and decided that it was time to do this. My heart was trying

to stop me from trying to be normal again. I need to think with my

head and not my heart. I take a deep breath and forced myself to

walk through the door. Everything looks the same as when my

mom left it. Even though it hasn't been open in months it still

looked really clean which was a good thing. I looked around the

place that seems so full, but so empty at the same time. First thing I

notice is that it could use a new paint job. The building used to be

white, but it had taken on a very grey tinge. A lot of their friends

had set up candles, teddy bear, etc. in memory of my parents. It

was sweet of them to do. I guess I'm not the only one who misses

them. There is even a police teddy bear for my dad. I feel bad I

might have to throw them away – but then again I might find a nice

spot for them to go to.

I walked slowly around the counter. My mom kept a larger butcher's knife under the counter just in case there was a robbery. I always told her that bullets move faster than a knife. She wouldn't be able to stop a bullet. I turn around to the wall and saw that she had our most recent family photo taped to the wall. I do miss her so much, hell I miss both of them if I'm being honest. I immediately stop pity party that I was about to throw myself. I took innovatory of everything that we had in the store. I needed to order more new snacks and convenience items as some things had expired after been on the shelf unsold for so long. After all the sweeping, mopping, and dusting for a few hours my bed was the only thing that I wanted. It was a long day of reopening the store, I look around and feel that I could do this. It was time to do what needs to be done otherwise what's the point of having the store around. Even though I have grown up in this store and the memories that I have, both good and bad, I still can't let Waters go.

I had got the store around seven in the morning and it well after noon by now. I really didn't expect a lot of people to show up on the first day of the reopen. I walked to the front of the store, turning on the open sign. Opening the store felt good, it felt like a piece of me was coming back to life. The decision to open the store was about me. It's about me reclaiming my power and my freedom to be able to live again. An hour or so went by and there was not a customer in sight. I turned around to reposition some of the memorial pieces that were left behind that I had decided to bring in the store. Then someone walked into the store I turned around to greet the customer.

"Hello, welcome to Waters how may I...Taika?!" I was stunned to see him.

I guess he doesn't understand what a breakup is. Per his sister, he's taking it hard. Towards the end he was a complete ass to me. It's for the best.

"Hey, Aquila, can I have a pack of cinnamon flavored gum?" He looks down the entire time afraid to look me in the eyes.

"Ok, one pack of gum? Your total is $1.15. Would that be cash or card?" I says grabbing the pack of gum that was sitting behind me on the self.

"Cash." He sits the money on the counter.

He proceeds to hand me the money and as he's about to walk out of the store Ki shows up. I still don't understand what the issue is between them is. Whatever it's it has nothing to do with me. Kiowa walks in with blue flowers in a white vase. They both just stare at each other for a minute or two but it felt like forever. Taika grabbed his pack of gum and looks at Kiowa before walking out the door. He didn't like Taika being around me before and even more so after my accident. There's something going on here I can't put my name on it yet. Kiowa watches him walk out the door and drive off. He breaks concentration with Taika then focuses on me.

"Hey, beautiful." He says happily.

"Hey! What was that about? There's a lot of tension in the room." I explain.

"Nothing, I don't like him being around you. He makes me nervous like he's going to do something to you." Ki says with concern.

"Well you have nothing to worry about. He just can't get over me for some reason." I say taking the flowers from him.

"I know. It's not you I'm worried about. Look, if he shows up again, please call me." He says with a stern look on his face.

"Kiowa…" He cuts me off.

"Trust me, ok." He says.

He looked at me with a half way smile. He turned to the door to check if Taika was going to come back. There's something he's not telling me and I desperately want to know what it is. I'm not going to ask, if it was something serious, I hope he would tell me eventually. I told Ki that I'm going to need his help fixing up the store. I put the flowers on the center of the counter behind me. They were one step into bringing the life back into the place.

I needed to talk to Kiowa anyway I have been thinking about the next steps for us. I want us to try living together before we get married. Marriage is a huge step for us - for anyone for the matter. In a normal perfect world, you date for a while then move in with someone before getting married. I have never lived with someone I have dated before. My relationship with Taika before all hell broke loose on my life was going nowhere. I think he was so lost about who he was that I somehow fell in love with him. Things became destructive toward the end of our relationship. There is no pint in helping someone who doesn't want to be saved.

Taika agreed with Alex when he made the joke about me being attacked by a bear. I was dealing with the most tragic moment of my life. I don't think I can forgive him for that one. I was at the most vulnerable and self-conscious version of myself at that time and he didn't care about that. My parents had died, my face was destroyed. I didn't think I needed to hear from someone who was that close to me judge me that harshly. Then he thinks it's all a joke and tries to play it off.

As I think about Taika randomly showing up at the store it makes me think that he's stalking me again – or maybe he never stopped. Out of all the stores in town, Waters was the only store you would be able to get gum from? This Taika and Kiowa beef that they have and no one wants to tell me what it's about. I could see it in Kiowa's eyes there's something that he's not telling me. They're both skipping around the truth.

I kept the store open for it normal hours. Surprisingly a lot of people came in once they realized that we were back in business. It's good to know that people are still willing to support. I don't think it would be hard for me to get back into a normal routine with the store.

Kiowa stays with me for the rest of the day. I mainly believe it's to make sure that Taika wouldn't come back. Since Ki was there he decides he was going to help with the store. Training him was fun, he had a joke for everything. I never ask him to come and help me he just did. No one is perfect, but maybe he is.

The next couple weeks Kiowa and I paint the store yellow. We also install some new brighter lights. You must be able give CPR when someone is drowning. I'm breathing new life into this place.

Deal with God

Dear God,

God, if you're here please hear me now. I come to you broken and scared. I don't know what I'm destined to do with my life. There are so many things that I would like for you to be able to answer, but I know that you can't. I have had so many people die in front of me. I don't think I can handle anymore.

I ask you to guide me and help me correct my wrong. I have so much to keep learning. God, if you can hear me understand I don't blame you for anything you have done.

I understand that I must take control of my life and my wellbeing. No one is going to be able help me fix what or change what happened in that car. I do regret what I said to my parents. It haunts me when I go to sleep at night. There are so many mistakes I have made that I don't know how or where to beginning to fix them. God, there are times that I thought I should have died in that car with them. I know you have a purpose for me. I just can't figure out what it is.

The day you chose to give me life is coming up. I want to make a deal with you. Hopefully by the end of this letter I understand what the deal is and I hope you will accept it. My mom and dad are gone, but I am here alive and slowly regaining my reason to be able to breath. I ask for you to protect me and my love ones.

As you may know I did blame you at first because you were the one pulling all the strings. I know you don't want to hurt me. God, I know you love me and care about me. I just need a sign that you love me and understand I mean no disrespect by this letter.

I guess what I'm trying to ask you is for a sign that I have nothing to be afraid of. I'm getting back into the swing of things. I don't want to go back to that person I was a couple of months ago. God, I'm afraid I'm going to lose someone that I love so much. I don't want to attend any more funerals.

In a year, I'm going to get married. I will be someone's wife. That says a lot about the future for me. I'm going to eventually have a kid. There so much fear in my heart. I have known Kiowa for so many years and the thought of losing him or hating him hurts. For Kiowa, his dad divorced his mom and he has not talked to him in years. My parents, instead of growing old together, they were growing to hate each other. I don't want us to have a child to grow up and realize that their parents hate each other. I had to deal with so much fighting that I felt so uneasy around them.

Not only would I be losing my husband I would be losing my best friend. I don't want to sound selfish, but I don't want to grow and hate him. My child shouldn't have to grow up with the same problems I had to go through. Maybe I'm over thinking what's going to happen in my future. God please hear me. I'm still trying to figure out how I'm going to go on without knowing if I and he are going to make it.

I still don't understand what happened to my parents to make them start hating each other so much. I can't remember where it went wrong, or where everything started. There are too many questions that I need the answers to and you can't give them to me.

I have had too many incidents with death. I know that everyone is going to die eventually. Sometimes I wish I had died a couple of months ago. I don't really care about my face anymore, but I feel like I'm dammed. I feel like I'm useless now. What good am I to anyone? I'm starting to think Ayana was right, a part of me did die in that accident.

The part of me that died was my sense of wonder, joy, and all-around caring. Life for me now is about taking a risk, as it should be. God I'm having trouble finding out who I am and what I am to do when things go bad again.

So, God If you read this letter. My deal is this if I am to die, please let me. Don't let anyone save me. If it's another car accident, let me go. I don't think I have it in me to go through another windshield and survive. If I am to live and die at 90. I ask of you to forgive me for my sin. I ask of you to watch over my children and protect them. Cover them in your blood and save them. If I am to die young, I ask of you to protect Kiowa and his family. My death would be too much for his heart to handle. His mom and brother would be able to grieve and move on but he wouldn't be able to. God this is my deal with you.

To: God

From: Aquila Waters

I place my letter in the small brown box that I keep in my closet. The box was my grandmother's that I took when she died. The box is where I keep everything that is important to me. It's not like we know what going to happen in the future. I just want God to know that I'm OK with whatever he decides to do.

Worthy of Trust

Friday night and I have the house to myself for a little while. Kiowa must help Ms. Maddox clean up the yard. That could take forever seeing how they have such a large property. I sat on the couch watching a scary movie. Right when the unmask killer was about to be revealed my doorbell rings. I always get interrupted at the best part. I look through the window and it was Taika. What part of *stay away from me* doesn't he understand? I knew how the conversation was going to go so I went ahead and open the door.

"Hey." I say wondering why he was there.

"Hey." He says looking agitated.

"Taika, what are you doing here? You're lucky Kiowa's not home otherwise he would freak out." I say grabbing my jacket.

"Aquila, there something you need to understand that I haven't told anyone. I do owe you a huge apology for everything. There's just something you need to know about me." He says.

"Ok, so explain." I say as I step outside to the porch and folding my arms.

"I have been with a lot of girls in my short life. Aquila, there is something special about you I can't seem to shake. I have been with so many girls that I can't even remember how many girls I been with! I admit I wasn't the best boyfriend to you. I do deserve to have you not to ever talk to me again! Aquila, I didn't go to graduation because I saw no point in being there. Did I really accomplish anything in life? If it wasn't for you helping me when I did decide to do my work I would have failed!" He says walking down the stairs from the porch.

"Taika..." I try talking but he cut me off.

"No, let me finish. I want to know why you were ever interested in me? I'm such an ass I drove you away. My mom being an alcoholic and beating me until she passes out. I don't think I can take much more of it, Aquila. Two weeks ago she hit Ayana with a bottle and she was passed out on the floor for a couple of hours." He says standing at the bottom of the steps.

"Taika, you don't have to tell me any of this. You don't owe me anything. Why are you telling me all of this now?" I ask.

"I need you to know so that you don't hate me or I don't leave a bad memory for you. I need one less person who I have some sort of relationship with to hate me. My mom has done so much damage I don't think she realizes what she has done to us. She drinks so much. I don't think she understands the repercussion of her actions. I think that she has turned me into damaged goods. Aquila, I wonder every single day what did I do in my previous life to deserve such a horrible life! My dad died when I was five, so I really don't have much memory of him. That could be the reason why my mom drinks so much." He says starting to elevate his voice.

"Taika, just stop already." I say trying to calm him down.

"Aquila, I don't even call her mom anymore. I stopped doing that a long time ago. She doesn't care about me or Ayana. All Fenna cares about is her bottle. If it was left up to her we wouldn't have food in the fridge. She would happily let us starve to death just so she can drink."

"Taika, please stop telling me this." I shout. But he doesn't listen he just keeps going on and on.

"The only way Fenna gets any money is by going out there and selling herself every single night!! She's probably slept with most of the men in Ruben. I can't tell you how many times we must bail her out of jail? How many times do I have to keep replacing all the things she has broken around the house? There were a couple of close calls that if Ayana hadn't calmed me down I don't know what I would do. I know a guy isn't supposed to hit a woman, but can someone please lock me in a room for five minutes with her!!" He yells kicking his car door.

"You are working yourself up, Taika. Stop it and calm down!" I scream.

"Ayana gets it the worst she doesn't fight back. She hopes one day that Fenna would be a loving mother again. She doesn't realize that *mother of the year* is too far gone. There is no turning back for her. Hell, why do I have to keep the house clean, buy groceries, and look after her? I don't know what it's like to have a good caring mother that loves you. Fenna doesn't care if I got hurt or if I'm dead. The Council of Elders is really what I consider family, they are truly my family. They take care of everyone in the

tribe." He yells.

"Taika, I'm sorry." I say while he continues on with his

tirade.

"Ayana is the only good thing I have in my life. Just Fenna

came back this morning drunk and badly beaten. Her face was

swollen I could barely recognize her. Apparently, her so called

client wasn't satisfied with the "service" he got and beat her.

Ayana had to clean her up. Even when asking her what happened

and the guy's name, she was too drunk to tell me. Most likely she

doesn't even know his name. If he did tell her a name it's probably

a fake one. Aquila, she started beating Ayana for trying to help her.

All she was trying to do was get the blood out of her hair and whip

her face off. I grabbed her and yelled at her. She only will listen

when someone is yelling at her. I let her hit me out of the ounce of

respect I have for her. However, I will not allow her to hit and ruin

Ayana. She doesn't deserve any of this, we don't deserve this.

Ayana called the ambulance to get her help. They come to our

house so often I think we should be friends. They get her clean, but as soon as she's back home the drinking begins again. This is hell but this is my life, Aquila." He cries.

"Taika, you never said anything about what you were going through. I would have helped you. I'm sorry you're going through all of that. Your mother set you up for failure and I can't begin to tell you how sorry I am for you. I don't know how to tell you how to fix it. Things are making sense to me in terms of what happened in our relationship. The way you used to talk to me is because of your mother. That doesn't excuse your behavior but it makes sense why you did what you did. You have never been loved by a woman. I'm sorry, Taika." I say feeling bad for him.

"Aquila, I was hoping that you would be the second good thing in my life but I ruined that. Can you forgive me?" He cries.

"I'm not God. I'm a human with emotion and I can only forgive so much. If God can show mercy, I guess I can. For the last time, Taika, I forgive you. This is my last time at giving you a chance at my mercy." I walk over and give him a hug.

"Thank you, Aquila. I appreciate it." He says.

"Ok, you need to leave before Kiowa shows up." I say.

Taika gets back in his car and drives off. I went back in the house feeling bad for him. I sure hope he doesn't ruin his last chance in me showing mercy for him. We will just have to wait and see.

Bluebird

The month of the store being opened was good. It felt good knowing that I could get back into the swing of things. A lot of the old customers came back, of course I got the "oh I'm sorry for your loss". I understood that people were being nice. I sort of wished they would just stop saying it. I knew that in time people would forget about the accident, but for me the wounds were still fresh. It takes time for a person to heal from the death of their parents. I know everyone misses them too. The accident happened months ago, but in my mind I knew it was time to start moving on. Funny thing is I feel like a whole new person – my perspective is different.

I have enjoyed my time being able to heal and grow as a person. In every situation that happens to everyone there is a lot of beauty that comes from it. In my case I learned how to love myself. Also, I found out how much pain I would be able to take on. Kiowa did have a lot to do with that, I give him credit for that. Otherwise, I would probably be depressed and losing my mind. It's so weird. Being with him is the best thing that could ever happen to me. It's funny how I'm going to marry my best friend. Since Waters has been open I have been forgetting to talk to him about moving in. He sat aside some time for us to go on a date after I close the store today and he got off work. It's the perfect time for us to just sit and talk.

Hours go by and it's my favorite time of the day closing time. I started restocking the store which takes up a lot more time than it should. I'm very particular when it comes to cleaning and organizing the store. In my head, everything has its place. It's rare that things are switched around in the store. Since we have the same customers all the time, plus we get tourist during vacation seasons there's no need to change. It's funny to me that I own the whole store. I can redo the store if I wanted.

I was almost done mopping the floor when Kiowa shows up to the store. Originally, I was supposed to meet him at Sal's for dinner. I had my back turned so I couldn't see him. He scares the crap out of me when I saw him. He could have knocked on the door instead of just standing there and waiting for me to see him. It's creepy of him to do that, it's not like I had on headphones and couldn't hear anything.

"Sorry, sir, we are closed for the night. We will be open tomorrow morning at seven o'clock." I smile holding the door.

"Well then you just lost a customer." He smiles romantically.

"I just lost one and gained three more." I laugh.

"Really, that's funny I'm supposed to be taking a beautiful girl out for a date tonight." He laughs.

I opened the door and let him in the store. It didn't make sense for him to come and meet me at the store when he himself told me to meet him at Sal's. In his own Kiowa way, he's very charming. He wants to drive me in his car, but I didn't feel comfortable leaving my car there so I decided following behind him in my car.

We drive to Sal's and I was so hungry I hadn't eaten anything all day. The store has been busy every day since I opened it back up. Seven months my parents had been gone from the earth, and in seven months I hadn't even drove on this street. The same street where my parents died and my life was forever changed. Ki wanted to go to Santos restaurant, but I want to get back to being somewhat normal, if at this point, that's even possible.

As I was driving I have a flashback and slam on the breaks quickly. Kiowa stopped his truck once he heard the breaks squeak. He was so scared that something had happened he pulls over and hops out his car running over to me. He looks so worried thinking something bad had happened. I got out of the car and walk over to the memorial that people had set up. The feeling of hunger had gone away and was instead replaced with a shit ton of anxiety. I took baby steps over to the bears and deflated balloons that were blowing in the wind. Even after all this time people were still paying their respects to my parents. I wasn't sad it's just the flash back to everything, I guess I'm still traumatized. I bent down to look at all the stuff that friends and people who felt bad about everything had left something to remember them by.

"Aquila, are you OK?" Kiowa places his hand on my back.

"Yeah, I'm fine. I haven't been down this road since the accident." I say holding onto one of the bears.

"We can head home I'll cook something for you to night." Ki says bending over to me.

"No, I'm fine we can head to Sal's. Plus I really want a
Hawaiian burger and fries." I say with a fake smile.

He didn't want me to drive I told him I was fine. I could
drive and that he should trust me. The knot in my stomach starts to
loosen up once I start driving away. Like I says, I hadn't been
anywhere near this area in the months since my parents' death.

Kiowa was still taking the lead. Once we got to Sal's and
we both were out of our cars Ki stops me to make sure that I was
OK. I told him that I was fine. He knew that I wasn't but he let it
be. Walking up the brick stone pathway into the restaurant Kiowa
was holding my hand while we were going into the restaurant. My
heart was beating so fast I thought it was going to pop out of my
chest. Kiowa opens the door for me and I walk through the door.
Sal's hasn't changed a bit. Since I used to go there every
Wednesday with my parents they knew exactly who we were. The
waitress who seated us was the same woman who was the start of
the argument. Funny how she has no clue that she was the root to
the accident. While she was taking our order the whole time I
noticed that people were staring at me. It was almost like I have a

huge sign that says look here. My hair was in a high ponytail that I quickly removed. I let my hair fall covering some of my scars.

Sal came out when he noticed I was there and decides to greet me. Sal was this older gentleman who was about in his late sixties, early fifties and he had a beer belly. He was funny cracking jokes and making us laugh.

"So glad to see you back in Sal's, Aquila. We miss you around here. I know you're probably tired of hearing this but I'm sorry for your loss. Your parents were very good people and friends. They're truly missed. Tell you what, since you're back in here for your first time anything you two order are on the house." Sal says with the kindness of his heart.

"Sal, you don't have to do that really." I say shaking my head.

"No, I insist on it." He says with a big smile.

To not seem ungrateful, I take the offer. I know he probably only did it because he feels sorry for me, I still felt bad accepting it. After we place our order and Sal left, Kiowa just looks at me. I look at the family sitting across the room their son, who had to be five, was staring at me. The mom turned him around and I assumed told him that it's not polite to stare at people. I could only hope that people don't stare at me. Soon, and real soon, I should become numb to the staring. Kiowa kissed the right side of my face were the scars are. I think he could sense that people were staring at me and that I was very uncomfortable. I turn looking at him with those big brown eyes.

"Kiowa, why do you always do that? You know kiss me on my bad side?"

"What bad side? I see nothing wrong with you." He looks me in my eyes.

"You know what I'm talking about. The side of my face that looks like it was attached by a tiger." I sighed.

"Quil, I want you to know something. I have loved you for longer than I think you even know. Look, don't think I just started having feelings for you just because I felt sorry for you. My mom was working the trauma unit the night of the accident. The paramedics called the hospital ahead of time to let them know a huge accident had just happened. I was on the phone with my mom, for what must have been a couple minutes, before you had arrived. Aquila, right before I hung up the phone the ambulance brought you into the trauma unit. My mom screams your name, she told me you were in an accident. She later told me when you arrived you were unresponsive and they didn't know how bad the damage was. All she knew that it was you covered in blood. She had no idea what happened to your parents. Aquila, once I heard that you were in an accident I couldn't believe what I had heard. I rushed to the hospital as fast as I could. I was a nervous wreck it, maybe took me twenty minutes to get there, but it felt like forever. The entire time I thought my heart was going to jump out of my chest.

"I waited for you to get out of surgery for four hours. I stayed the entire night until the next day when you woke up. That night I made two promises to myself. The first promise is that I need to make sure you are safe and out of harm's way. The second is to not keep my feelings about you hidden anymore. Aquila, I have been in love with you for a while now. I thought that night you were gone. The reason I'm so protective over you is because I can't stand the thought of losing you. That night made me realize how much I truly love you." He gives me a look that I had never seen before. I wipe the tears away from his face.

"I can see why you didn't tell me before. Since we are being honest with each other I had feeling before too. I was scared that things would be different with us being together. I didn't want us to become like our parents. I didn't want to hate you. I was scared I was going to lose my best friend. Kiowa, we grew up together we have seen each other go through hell and back. Maybe we were meant to be with each other. Ki, I kind of had a feeling about the unspoken things between us. We've danced around it for years without saying a thing about it to each other. I started noticing when you were being over protective of me when it came to Taika. I thought it was just you being a friend and not someone who loved me more than that. I guess I gained much more than that, you know having you in my life." I say wiping the tears from my eyes.

"We both did." He says.

"Kiowa, we are going to be getting married and I want to know if you would like to move in with me?" I look at him giving him a set of keys and the bottom lock to garage while I wait for a response.

"Yes, of course I will." He says taking the keys. I laugh to myself a bit because it was almost as if I was proposing to him.

The waitress brings us our food and we eat, trying to have a good normal date night. It's a good thing that we are able to get a lot off our chests. I have come to realize that I'm growing up. There are somethings that we aren't going to be able to change. I don't want my life from this point on to be some sad story. Maybe adding a bit of positivity into my daily routine could help. The last seven months were hell I admit, but I don't want the next seven years and beyond to be like that.

After we were done eating and left the restaurant we drive back in separate cars. Kiowa wants to drive behind me this time. He wants to make sure that I don't freak out again and end up in yet another accident. We get to what used to my house to our house, it feels so natural. We agreed that we didn't want our parents' tragic marriages, so if things get rough we need to fix them before we begin hating each other. I tell him that I want to clean out my parents' room. I didn't want to move into their room because that would make me feel awkward. I just didn't want to deal with any evil spirits that were in there that were left over from my parents. Not to mention the fact that they slept in that room and again weird as shit. It just dawns on me that it's like we will be giving birth to a new life between us. All I can ask for is that things stay normal for a while.

Silent Scream

I was finally glad that Ki told me how he found out that I was hurt. A couple days later I had a dream about the night. I think going to Sal's made the memories come back up. It was like I was Kiowa that night of the accident. My dream started out with Kiowa waiting for his mom to get home. Ms. Maddox is the hardest working woman I know. I mean it's a hospital, it's not like it's an everyday job. Funny how Kiowa used to wish that she would work a nine to five job. I guess that's the price of being a doctor. The night sky wasn't bright like it normally is. The stars must be taking the night off. Koda, Kiowa's brother, was out late with a bunch of his friends. Knowing how Ms. Maddox is he's lucky she wasn't home. The week before Koda was placed on punishment for starting a food fight.

It felt weird being in Kiowa's head the night of the accident I don't know why God had given me the insight into his dreams. It was getting very late I guess Kiowa called his mom to verify if she's doing a double. He was hoping that she's would not be in surgery so he could talk to her. I walked closer to Kiowa so I could hear the conversation. I waved my hand in front of his face. He couldn't see me, I was a ghost.

"Mom, how's it going? Are you working another double again?"

"Sadly, yeah I am son, we just received a call there was a huge car accident. The paramedics said that it's bad. So, I don't know how long I'll be." She sighed.

"Mom, you have been working so hard I…" As he was talking the screams from his mother cuts him off.

"Oh, my goodness, Aquila!! Kiowa, Aquila was the one in the car accident I got to go." She screams and hangs up the phone.

I know this is a dream but I have never seen Kiowa this scared since I've known him. I am talking so scared to the point where I could feel ever beat of his heart. He drops the phone and had to take a breath. He stood there for a second not knowing what to do. There aren't any books on how to handle situations like this. I have never seen Kiowa so panicked before. He grabs his keys and races out the door. I follow him to the car. Koda pulls up and was walking up their stairs. He asks why Kiowa was in such a rush.

Kiowa told him about huge car accident. He was praying that I was OK as he was heading to the car. I could hear him talking to himself asking God to protect me.

Kiowa knew that his mom was my doctor. He had faith that she would do anything to keep me alive. As Kiowa arrives at the hospital there was so much fear in his heart. He had no idea how to handle any of this. He just sat in the waiting room for hours for me to get out of surgery. The entire time I watch him pray for me to be OK. The nervous look on his face lifts when he saw Ms. Maddox. He asks her a thousand questions.

"How is she? What happened? Did you get a chance to call her parents?" He asks in a panicked voice.

"Kiowa slow down. The paramedics says when they arrived on seen the car was on fire. Aquila had gone through the windshield somehow. She will be OK physically, but it will take some time for her to heal mentally. Son, her parents were still in the car when it was on fire they died." She says with sorrow in her voice.

"Mom, I need to see her!" He cries out.

Ms. Maddox walked him back to recovery area. All he was thinking was how he could have lost his best friend tonight. Being able to see him in the dream shows me just how much more to him I mean than I realize. Ms. Maddox leaves him alone with me. I had gauze wrapped around my face he could barely see me. He grabs my hand holding it in his.

He looks at me so endearing. "Aquila, you have no idea how much I love you. It has taken me so long to say that to you without feeling afraid. You will never have to worry about anything with me. I promise I'm going to keep you safe. Just know that your parents, as much as they pissed you off, will always be with you no matter what. I know you're just getting out of surgery and can't hear me, you are the most beautiful thing in the world to me and you don't even know it. Have you ever felt your heart skip a beat because you love someone so much you're scared to lose them?" He says kissing my hand and crying.

He stays with me that night hoping, watching, and praying that I would be able to make it through – just as he says when he told me when we were at Sal's. He knew that he was going to have to tell me what happened to me and my parents. I could tell that he had never had so much of the world on his shoulders than he did that day.

As I begin to think on it, I'm wondering if parts of this dreams is actually parts that I remember in my subconscious. Maybe I remember him sitting at my bedside but I happened to block everything out? I woke up out of my dream with Kiowa's arms wrapped around me. I wonder how in this moment he was the love of my life and I didn't even know it. I was the one to bear the worst of the situation, but he never left me alone.

Sight of the Sun

I have been so focused on running the store that I haven't really had time for myself. Lilly texts me last night about a party she was having and invites me to come by. She's throwing this last minute party as a going away event because she'll be leaving to go off to college. I didn't mind going because honestly, I didn't think it would be more than five of us, our circle was a little small during high school. I told her that I would come. I'm starting to feel older than I'm looking and it's time to be young for once in my life. The party was going to be four hours before sunset on the beach today. It's just a bunch of our former classmates. It feels like a mini after graduation reunion, it has felt good not having to see the same people every day - not saying that I hate everyone. Toward the end of school everything was just boring and we all know I was just over it. But after taking a break I was happy to see a few people.

I have struggled with being a girlie-girl my entire life. I'm trying to change that about myself. The thing is I'm comfortable in jeans, sweatpants, and a t-shirt with a funny saying on it. Trying to dress up, put on makeup, you know the whole girlie thing is the most painful thing that I can ever do. I'm going to be positive about everything and go shopping and to find something cute for the party today. Since it's at the beach shopping should be quick and easy. How hard will it be to find a swim suit? The answer to that is very hard, even though I'm not a girlie-girl, I'm a woman and can't make up my mind. I decide to go to Feather's they have a variety of different styles that will help me find something more within my personality.

As I'm shopping I realize how much I'm really going to miss Lilly. She's one of those friends that makes her mark on everyone. She's like a sickness that you can never get rid of. No matter how much you try it's still there – I know it sounds bad but that's just how much of an impression she leaves on people. That's why I love her, she's one of those people who you don't want to get rid of.

Normally when I go shopping I'm just used to picking up items and leaving the store. I rarely have to try on anything. Today was just an entirely different story. I was looking around at everything trying to make up my mind just which swim suit I should try on. There were a lot of cute suits on some of the racks that caught my eye. It took me a minute to realize that they only have bikinis and not a one-piece swim suits. Living in the twentieth century I'm starting to find it hard to find clothes that cover. This has nothing to do with my accident and my face being scared up. This has everything to do with the fact that I like dressing modestly. In the modern world, it's starting to get hard to do that.

I have no option but to go with a bikini or the other option is not attend the party - which I'm not trying to do. I start to look through the rack of bikini's one after the other. The more I look through the racks the smaller the suits get and the more skin they show. I found a *normal one*, if that's what you can even call it. The bikini was black with a push up bra top that ties together. The entire time I must worry about my chest falling out. If that happens I would drown myself. The bottoms were going to be a nightmare. The designer couldn't make them plain basic bottoms? No, they had to cut the sides out so its looks like stings holding everything together. I'm short on time so I just go with a semi-simple one that I see.

I leave the swim wear section to go pay for my things. As I'm making my way to the register, I notice the lounge wear clothing section. I figured I could get a nice cover up to wear over my bikini and something else more comfortable for later. As I was going through the racks there was a night set that I thought would be a nice gift I could surprise Ki with once he was all moved in, or even our wedding night. If you could even call it a night set, the extremely short gown was completely see through. It came with a push up bra and a thong. Even though I thought it was the craziest thing I could have ever thought of spending my money on I still bought it. After getting making up my mind on the other items I head to the line to before I spent too much money on items I didn't need.

As I stand in line, one thing I will always notice is when someone is staring at me. There were two teenagers standing behind me just staring at me. I could feel their eyes on me out of the corner of my eye. One of the girls was whispering to the other girl about me. They both were tall and look like they could be sisters. One of the girls has black short hair that was pulled into a high ponytail. She seems the most fascinated about what happened to me, the other girl couldn't care less. If I were to guess they appear to be about sophomores in high school. Although, I'm used to it, the staring doesn't bother me, but I still think it's still rude. Even the cashier was staring at me the entire time as she was tending to customers in ahead of me in line.

I was happy to finally be out of the store and on my way home. As I drive home I have to fight the urge to stay at home and get in the bed. But I need to change into the bikini and make the drive to the beach. As I go into the house Kiowa is sitting at the living room table. I hide the bag of clothes behind me, as if he didn't see them already. I had forgotten I had given a key to him, seeing how I have been living alone for the last seven months. Funny, I now must get used to living with someone again. He was stopping by to bring some of his things over. I had texted him earlier to tell him that I was going to Lilly's going away party.

Kiowa stayed downstairs as I walk up the stairs to go and change my clothes. I rush pass my parents' bedroom subconsciously ignoring it like I always do. For some reason I continued to keep my parents' bedroom door closed. I saw no need to go in there, but I know that I needed to start packing their things away. Part of it is my laziness, but the other part of me is just trying to avoid it. But I'm determined to get around to cleaning in a day or two. It's weird saying I'm getting married soon. And the funny thing is that door probably would have stayed closed for another two years if Ki wasn't moving in with me.

I go into my room and get dressed. I personally inspect myself in the mirror. I look good in the bikini after finally really giving myself a once over, but I still would prefer to be covered up a little bit more. I grab my backpack and head back downstairs. Kiowa was moving things around when I came down. I told him that I was leaving. He turns around to see that I had on only the bikini, my dress that I was going to put on over it was in the basement hanging up on the clothing line. His eyes became tremendously large, at the end of the day he still a guy and is a visual creature.

"Quil, you look amazing as always. But since I'm your fiancé, do I get a say so in your outfits? I don't want anyone thinking they can talk to you." He laughs and walks over to me and kisses me.

"I believe someone is jealous." I laugh at him.

"No, I think every guy is jealous of me. They're jealous because I have the most beautiful and talentedly ambitious women in the world that's going to marry me. They're mad because they can only dream about having a woman like you." He looks at me dead in my eyes and smiles.

"I think we are both lucky. I'm blessed to have one of the sweetest men in the world." I smile and kiss him. I run down to the basement to get my dress before Ki walks me to my car.

I made my way to La Plano Beach where Lilly was having her party. Plano is the quietest beach in the world. Hardly anyone ever comes to that beach which is why it's the perfect beach for a small intimate party. It's one of the places I go to walk around, it's the perfect place to go clear your head and relax. This beach is special to me. After the accident this beach helped me get out of the depressed state that I was in on plenty of days, not to mention it's were all my most embarrassing moments have happened. My mom, dad, Lilly, Kiowa, and Ms. Maddox all made memories as this beach. I remember when we were kids we came down to the beach and were playing in the water and a jelly fish that stung me. I completely lost my mind and I made all the adults freak out. My mom almost had a heart attack she was so scared. My dad just so happened to have his police cruiser there as well and made a big spectacle out the situation and drove me to the hospital with his sirens blaring. Ms. Maddox had called ahead to the hospital and had everything prepped before we even arrived. All because of a jelly fish sting. To this day Lilly will never let me forget it. I was perfectly fine but everybody made a big fuss about it.

I arrived at the beach a little early and Lilly was already there trying to set things up. She stops what she was doing and runs over to my car. She acts like she had never seen me before a day in her life. She grabs my hand and pulled me over to the beach. I instantly sit down on one of the logs. She didn't even let me catch my breath and was already trying to shove a beer in my face. I decline the beer and grab a bottle of water instead. Lilly made fun of me for choosing the water instead. She decides to tease me by giving me a new nickname and calls me *grandma*. I didn't let it bother me though. I told her I needed to drive home but that doesn't stop her from making fun of me.

Hours goes by and we all having fun the party grew a little larger than Lilly was anticipating but it was all in fun. Josh brings out a football and all the guys join in a game of tag football. One thing I loved to do is get in the water so I decided to take a few dips. When I'm in any body of water I feel so free. Water, no matter how small or big, allows you to be free. When I'm in the water I forget all about my struggles and what's going in my life. I stay in the water for a bit just thinking, letting your mind wonder about my future. Josh swims by me and completely submerged me underwater, lucky I know how to swim. His plan failed in trying to scare me, I got out from his grip and was able to flip him under water. He was so pissed. I told him don't mess with the junior life guard and laugh at him. I got out of the water and went to sit on the log and eat. Surprisingly, I wasn't ready to leave yet, I was having fun.

I liked that I could chill and hang out for a bit, I have had so much going I didn't think I have taken the time out to enjoy my life. Life still had to go on and I didn't have to leave under a dark cloud just because my parents were gone. Everyone stayed and watches the sun set, then the beach party turned into a bonfire. The others were drinking, I still stuck to my plain water and occasional soda. Everyone was calling me a square, but I didn't let it bother me - I was fine with that. I have a forty-five minute drive going back home. I wanted to be smart so I can make to see Ki. One thing about my friends when they're drunk is they say whatever is on their mind. Josh was so drunk he was already passed out. It was only Joseph, Lilly, Mark, and Beverly left awake.

"Aquila, come on have a drink with us. Don't be such a grandma." Joseph says as he was falling over himself.

"No, I'm good. I have to drive home."

At this point I was looking at everyone. I notice that the guys were getting a little too drunk and out of hand.

"Hey guys leave her alone. You know Kiowa will have your neck for disrespecting Aquila like that." Lilly laughs.

"I don't need Kiowa's help. I'm taking good care of myself now." I look at them and laugh.

"Yea, she could have used Kiowa's help when that jelly fish stung her." Lilly says and laughs at me.

"I'm going to get you for that Lilly!" I hop up and run after her for teasing me.

I was so out of breath after chasing Lilly, what I can say the girl is fast. I'll have to tackle her some other time. We rejoin the group, this was when my old lady habits kicks in. I grabbed my backpack, my water bottle, and headed to my car to go home. I drank the rest of my water while Lilly walks me to my car. I start driving home and I turn on the radio - the news station was on. The news was sort of depressing it seem like all over the world something bad was happening. Suddenly, out of nowhere, I start getting sleepy and nauseated. I could barely even see the road. My vision was starting to disappear. I pull the car over and stumble out. I begin to vomit all over the place. I tried to get up and call for help, but I was no longer able to even stand up.

There was a car coming up the road I couldn't see anything, the only thing I could see was the head lights. To my surprise it was Taika and Ayana. Usually I would not have wanted to see them, but on this day I couldn't be happier to see them. Ayana was asking me if I was OK. I didn't know what was happening to me it was like my body was dying. I was wondering if it was something that I had eaten or did something accidently stick me and I was having a bad reaction to it.

Taika and Ayana decide to help me and get me off the side of the road. Ayana drives my car to my house to get Ki and Taika puts me in the front seat of his car and takes me to the hospital. He's asking me all types of questions about what's wrong with me but I don't know how to answer because I don't know either. Honestly, I couldn't even hear him clearly because I was out of it.

Taika and I arrive at the hospital, it's a shame that I know this place all too well. If I never see another hospital again I would be happy. Since I was in the hospital so long after my accident a lot of the nurses knew who I was. Everyone was looking concerned. Everyone was asking me what had happened but I wasn't even able to tell them because I didn't know myself. I eventually passed out, my body gave in.

The next morning I wake up still in the hospital and Taika was there waiting for me to wake up. I was happy that he and Ayana were driving by and helped me out. I was wondering why Taika was there all night and Ki wasn't there. I was still a little bit out of it but I want my phone so I could call Kiowa and Ms. Maddox. I wasn't sure that they were aware of what had happened to me. This was weird being in this similar situation all over again.

"Hey, Taika. Thank you for helping me. I really appreciate it." I say awkwardly.

"No problem. But you should be more careful drinking and driving. Haven't you been in enough car accidents for one person?" He says smiling and scolding me at the same time.

"Taika, I wasn't drinking. I don't know…" I was cut off when Kiowa came in.

"Quil, are you ok? What happened?" He says panicky.

"I'm fine now. I don't know what happened. I don't really remember much." I try to calm him down.

"She lucky we were driving by to save her. Seeing how she was in bear country things could have been a lot worst." Taika says looking at me.

"Taika, thank you. I really do mean that." I look at him and smile.

"Thank you. You can go now. She's safe with me now. I can take care of her." Kiowa tells at Taika. I was slightly embarrassed. Instead of Ki being grateful that Taika was there to help me he was being in his feelings.

"Why are you acting like you can be the only one who can take care of her. She's a grown woman. I think she can handle herself without you. Also seeing how you weren't around she was by herself I don't think you were doing a good job at that." Taika yells back.

"Could both of you stop arguing. You both have saved me multiple times. I thank you both for that, can we move on from this." I yell at them.

"Well seeing how she is my fiancé and soon to be my wife, it's my job to protect her." Ki says in Taika's face.

"You're marrying him?! Here are your keys, Aquila. I'm leaving." Throwing my key on the bed, Taika storms out of the room. He slams the door so loud I think my heart skips a beat.

There're certain moments when I wish I was dead. This is one of those moments were death would have been better than facing this situation. Taika and Ayana both saved my life, I could have effortlessly crashed the car. There's also the fact that a bear could have killed me as well.

After all the commotion calms down the emergency room doctor finally came back with information about what happened to me. Apparently there were drugs in my system. There's a new drug that people are using to get high called ENT. According to my nurse I had so much in my system it could have easily put two horses down. I was shocked because I was trying to think back on when someone would have had the time to drug me. It definitely happened at the Lilly's party but I'm trying to figure out when exactly. After they pumped my stomach and clear of any residue of the drug I was allowed to go home.

Ms. Maddox drives us to their house, Kiowa really didn't make any conversation. I know that he was still mad. His mom tries to get him to talk, I don't think she really understands the level of hate those two have for each other. She pulls up to the house, Kiowa gets out the car and opens the door for me. Kiowa is very sweet, but he can be a hard ass sometimes. When he's upset he will surely let you and anyone else know. Ms. Maddox starts talking about her plans for the wedding. I can see he didn't tell her

we are waiting a year. She starts telling about colors, dresses, and

bows. See that all that just happened just last night, I really didn't

want to talk about the wedding. I was starting to get a bit

overwhelmed.

Their house is weird, the kitchen is the first thing you see

when you walk in the house. Ms. Maddox also has her house

stocked full of food. Her kitchen is like one big grocery store. She

offered me some fry bread she just made last night. She would

have cooked a whole meal for me if I didn't stop her. Luckily, she

had plans somewhere with her friends, Kiowa just stood in the

corner of the kitchen watching everything. She fixes a small plate

of food for me. According to her I'm going to be going through

withdrawals and food would be the best thing for me. She kisses

me on the forehead and heads out the door to go meet up with her

friends.

As she closes the door behind her I look over at Ki, he's

just starting at me. "I know there's something you want to say, Ki.

You look like you're about to explode." I stop eating and say.

"There's actually nothing, you should finish eating. Aquila, you need something on your stomach." He shakes his head.

"Kiowa, I know you're mad. How many years have we known each other? I can feel when you're upset. Don't try and change the subject, beside I'm not hungry anyway." I look at him.

"Aquila, Taika should not keep popping up like this." He slams his fist on the table.

"Kiowa, I didn't call him. Taika and Ayana found me lying on the ground. I could barely see anything. Taika is in the past for me. Don't you know that? I'm lucky he did find me otherwise I would be dead form an overdose. I love you and only you. Don't you know and believe that? Ki, I know you want to be the one who will always save me every time. The truth is you can't, you work, I work, and we are not together 24/7." I explain.

"That's about to change. I am moving in this week! I'm going to make sure that you are safe. I don't want him around you anymore." He walks away and heads up to his room.

Whoever says that males don't experience a menstrual cycle lied. It's not my fault that someone drugged me at the party.

How am I getting blamed for something I had no control over? I'm not going to try and find out who, there was no point. I'm trusting that Lilly had nothing to do with any of this.

Later on that evening Ms. Maddox came back home, she wasn't letting me go home tonight. I was planning on sleeping on the couch, Kiowa told me that I was sleeping in his room tonight. She says that I will have the worst time sleeping tonight. I have already started to have been cold sweats from the withdrawals. I don't understand how people do drugs if it makes you feel like that.

I decide to go sit out by the fire. The tension from Ki was still very thick. I could see Kiowa upstairs through the window taking things down and packing them in boxes. Koda, Ki's younger brother, decides to come and sit out with me. It's funny just how much he looks like Kiowa when he was younger, the only difference was the bushy eyebrow. He's in his junior year, but he still acts like a baby that needs to be taken care of, but I'm sure with time he'll grow up.

"Just so you know, Kiowa has been in love with you for years. I'm happy I don't have to hear about it anymore. He would come in the house everyday going on about how good you look, what you did or said on any given day. I happy you guys are together so I won't have to hear about it anymore. You know he doesn't know how to express his anger well. Oh, and don't tell him I told you any of this. Thanks to you I get to have his room now." He whispers over to me as we look at the fire.

Kiowa's was upstairs packing up everything. His room was the most organized thing I'd ever seen. He has boxes filled with his things piled up in the corner. He gave me a t-shirt and a pair of shorts to wear to bed. Like I say, when he is mad at you he will gladly let you know. I am still was feeling sick so I head to the bathroom because I thought I was going to vomit. The bathroom was close to Ms. Maddox's room. Her door was opened and she saw me go into the bathroom. After I gathered myself and came out of the bathroom, Ms. Maddox calls out to me to come into her room.

She lives in color, her room looks like a page out of a child's coloring book. The rest of the house was normal while her room was totally abstract. This is the first time I have ever been in her room. Even though it was loud with color it is still peaceful in its own way. Ms. Maddox wants to make sure that I'm aware of all that I will experience as the drug's effects wear out of my system. ENT is used to make people hallucinate and is also used as a date rape drug. The amount someone gave me was over the normal dose if someone was to consume it.

After talking to Ms. Maddox, I went back to Kiowa's room, I think he was determined to pack his entire room. I watch him for a couple of hours trying not to fall asleep box after box.

"Quil, you should be asleep by now. What are you still doing up?" He turns and looks at me, then proceeds to continue packing.

"I can't sleep." I say a sweaty mess.

"Alright I'm done for the night. I'll go sleep on the couch, see you in the morning. I want you to get some rest. " He stops packing the last box.

"Kiowa, I know you're mad at me, but be mad at me tomorrow. Tonight, I need you to sleep by me. Your mom says I will most likely have flashbacks of the accident again. I don't think you realize how scared I am to close my eyes and go to sleep tonight. Seeing we have already slept together there shouldn't be an issue with you being in the same bed with me. Protect me tonight, be mad at me tomorrow." Tears start rolling down my face. I couldn't bear going through that pain again.

Kiowa stops fumbling with the box and he turns back around to me. He takes off his shirt and puts on some basketball shorts and hops in the bed with me. I have never been so scared to fall asleep, my body temperature keeps rising and dropping. I didn't know what to do, there's nothing to I can do until the drug is out of my system. Kiowa told me he wasn't mad at me. He was mad at Taika. Ki told me he's just scared of losing me again. Hell, I'm scared of losing myself again.

We talk about random things to keep me distracted until I eventually pass out. I don't know how long I was sleeping for. I hated that Ms. Maddox was right. It seems like that night I relived the entire accident in my dreams. This time it feels like I was physically there in that moment again. I felt myself go through the window as the glass cuts me. The pain from me sliding on the asphalt, my bones breaking. I saw the car on fire and heard the screams from my parents burning alive in the car. I can smell there burning flesh. I woke up screaming at the top of my lungs, the dream felt so real. I was in hell all over again.

I hated whoever it was that drugged me. To go through looking at that scene in my dreams made me feel like I was looking at the devil face-to-face. I woke the entire house up. Ms. Maddox and Koda came bursting through the door. They all were so worried about me. Kiowa yells at them to go away he would take care of me. I was sweaty and in tears, he pulls me close to him, holding me tightly. He let me just cry on his chest. I cry like a newborn entering the world. Have you ever felt a pain in your chest so bad that you can't breathe? I feel totally out of control.

I couldn't go back to sleep after that. I went outside and sat by the cliff watching the water. I couldn't bring myself to go back upstairs and sleep, whether it was a dream or not, it felt so real again. Kiowa gave me space before coming down to check on me. It's tricky not knowing what to do in a situation like this.

I had come so far with dealing with my parents' death. After clearing my mind I still planned on cleaning up my parents' room today. It was time to move on in life. I wasn't going to let this distraction consume me. Ki wraps me in a blanket with his arms around me to comfort me. Every nerve in my body was on high alert, I thought I was going to jump out of my skin.

"Quil, I'm so sorry I never meant to yell at you earlier." He rubs my shoulders.

"It's OK. Couples get into fights. It's normal. We have been with each other for almost a year with no fights."

"It's not OK. I let my own ego get in the way. I hate Taika for all the shit he has put you through in the past. I was mad at him yesterday because he could get to you before I could. I was mainly scared to lose you. I was in the wrong, I am sorry." Kiowa get on his knees facing me holding my hand in his.

We watch the sunrise together in silence. My fear had gotten the best of me because of the dream, but I was determined not to let it break who I am and what I'm working towards. Kiowa brought me back into the house and cooked breakfast for me. Ms. Maddox was awakened by the smell of the food. Kiowa made cinnamon blueberry pancakes and eggs - it smells good but I really didn't want to eat. His mom came downstairs in huge fluffy green robe, it was cute just too much fluff for me. She checks my eyes to make sure that my pupils didn't look like I had spaceships for eyes. I apologized for waking her and Koda up, but she didn't care she understood why I was going through what I went through. She starts going on about how much of a good man she raised her son to be. Ms. Maddox took a pancake and went upstairs to get ready for work.

Koda was wakened up by Ms. Maddox going on about me and Kiowa. She was happy that her son found the love of his life. Koda was happy that his big brother was leaving. Koda keeps bragging about what he's going to do the room now since it will be his. I sat back and watch both of them bicker over who had the best room. Koda eventually stops and goes upstairs, I assume he was getting ready for school.

Once everyone was gone Kiowa turns to look at me. He just looks sad worried even the more. I know he's concerned about the rough night I had. But I think I've done good seeing that I haven't had any flashbacks of the accident besides the night at Sal's. Last night didn't feel like a flashback. It felt like I was there again. I think everything happens for a reason and maybe I needed to relive it all over again just so I could move on. Ki and I finished what was left of breakfast so that I can get back to my house.

I made Kiowa drive me home. I was tired and stressed and I need to be in my home to rejuvenate myself. I love that Kiowa is going to move in with me. My plan is to turn this house of pain into a truly loving home. Almost like the things you see in movies, even though I know movies are fantasies but I was going to try to get as close to it as possible. But now that I was home the only thing I want right now was a shower and sleep the rest of the past events off.

I looked like an old wet dog on its last day alive. After I was done with my shower I get dressed in some pajamas and head downstairs. I looked at my parent's room. Even though I was tired I knew I wasn't going to be able to sleep without cleaning there room out. I push myself to enter into their room and just get it over with. It was cold and there was barely enough sunlight coming through the window. I run downstairs to retrieve a garbage can and some large bags to get things cleared out – it was now or never.

I don't know how long it took me to clean the room, and by cleaning I mean I was just throwing shit out – it was just some memories of them that I didn't want to deal with. Once I got into the groove it was no stopping me. I must have looked like a crazy person to anyone who drove by. This woman in her pajamas moving all of these items out of her house as if she's about to have a garage sale. I didn't want to keep anything, they really didn't have a lot of stuff to begin with. I can remember there would be a couple of fights that were so bad that my mom would go bat shit crazy and break everything. I throw away clothes, shoes, sheet sets, furniture, and even the mattresses. I don't know where the strength came from the eventually the entire room was completely empty.

What were left were the holes in the wall from their fights. I run downstairs to the dining room and living room. I look around and see other things that remind me of the negativity of my parents' marriage, I throw out anything that either started a fight or that they used to throw at one another. The study was the biggest room in the house, I moved the desk into what used to be my parents' room all by myself. I turned my parents' room my own private office and made the study my room. I'm starting things on a fresh piece of paper. If I am to be married, if I am to be loved, I have to do what I feel I need to do to have a normal marriage. Time to clear out all the negative omens in this house.

After I was done I feel better. I go downstairs and sit on the couch and went to sleep. I slept for the entire day after cleaning house. When I awoke Kiowa was there unpacking some of his things. I was so deep in sleep I didn't even hear him when he initially came in and started bringing in his boxes. I feel like there was a huge bolder being lifted off my head. I didn't feel bad anymore. Minus the fact that I was drugged two nights ago I feel completely new. I must be responsible of the life I'm attempting to rebuild and start. Kiowa had no idea I was up, I sat up on the couch, just watching him. His back was turned toward me so he couldn't see me stalking him like a wild animal. There were so many boxes all over the place it's unbelievable. After I had cleaned the house from top to bottom he messed it up again with all his boxes. I really think he packed all his belongings last night.

Eventually I get up because I know it will be time for dinner soon and I'm sure Ki will be hungry after all the work he's doing.

I startled Ki a little when I get up to talk to him. "Kiowa I'm going to cook some catfish. Have any ideas of a side to go with it?" I look at him with a smirk on my face.

"Nice to see you're doing OK. You don't have to worry about dinner tonight. My mom cooked so much food for us I think we are going to be set for a while. She still sees me as her baby boy. She's having a mini nervous breakdown about this move, but she'll be OK." Ki moves a box to the side and then comes sits by me. "I see you cleaned your parents' room while I was gone. How did you move all the furniture downstairs without hurting yourself?" He laughs.

"Your mom is so sweet. I'm glad she cooked for us. And you're forgetting I was on drugs, I don't know how I moved everything – I just did it. Also, there was a reason for all the madness. That room is going to be big enough for the both of us and then some. My old room we can just leave that empty until we can figure out what to do with it." I look at Kiowa, he was so confused.

"Ok. I still think you have some explaining to do. I mean you're getting stronger? I can't have you walking around here stronger than me. We have to talk." We both laugh.

We ate dinner together and watch TV. I believe once we get all settled and into a routine this will be a great thing for Ki and I. Kiowa has become my first in a lot of situations. Maybe the stars are aligning in the right direction for me. After dinner and some cuddle time on the couch we head to bed for the first time as couple in their own home. Not a house, but a home.

Gust of Wind

It's been a couple of weeks since Kiowa have moved in and I must say I enjoy it. I guess you can say we are in our unofficial newlywed stage. We have turned my parents' broken down house into our home. Kiowa was just promoted at work and I couldn't be happier for him. Not that we need the money, but it has been helping a lot with the redecorating. I have a house, I'm making it my own, well our own.

My crazy throwing everything out and switching room worked out. Kiowa's about to use the study to do work, which he could make himself a man cave if he wanted. We painted the kitchen a nice light brown color to make it brighter. The study was painted yellow with white trim. I did a complete redo of the bedroom, before the walls were a dark brown color. It took some convincing of Ki, but he finally agreed to paint the walls grey. I found a furniture store and got an eight-piece bedroom set for barely anything. The very place that I used to consider a hell hole was now my home.

My birthday was coming up and I have the perfect plan to do nothing. It's the most amazing idea ever, but if I know Ki like I think I know him, I'm sure he has something planned. I'm having never been big on birthdays, hell, I stopped counting years ago. Seeing how I was drugged for the first time in my life going out is not something that's on my mind now.

Another thing we have to get used to is seeing Ms. Maddox a lot. She hasn't gotten used to Kiowa being out of the house yet. And Koda is trying to adjust as well. He didn't realize how much his mom would start harassing him now that Ki was gone. In his words she's trying to smothering him. I keep telling him just give it time she will get used to it eventually – I'm sort of encouraging myself as well Ms. Maddox can be a bit overwhelming at times.

Ms. Maddox comes over almost every other day. I stole her son away from her so I don't mind her coming over – but I hope she get over it soon. But I can't complain much, she is like a second mom to me and it's nice to have someone around to be able to give you motherly advice and guidance when you need it.

Living with your parents is much different form living with your boyfriend. This has been the first time I have been living with someone since my parents' death. I must remember that if something goes missing Kiowa moved it somewhere. My thing when I come home is the undress and walk around the house in my underwear, before you judge me I work eight hour days and am on my feet for most. I think I deserve to be able to walk around my house in my underwear, but not to make him uncomfortable I wear pants – he's not as free as I am when it comes to that. The good thing about both of us is that we are very organized. I'm a clean freak and can't stand a lot of mess being everywhere. That stereotype about girl's rooms/houses being clean, but their cars being a mess is true, but that rule doesn't apply to me, my car is as clean as a sliver spoon.

As the evening went on you could hear the storm outside. The thunder was boisterous and I could see the flash of the lighting come through the window. It was the middle of the night I was completely dead asleep. There was a sudden knock on the door, it sounded like someone was going to break the door in. Ki was sound asleep he didn't hear the knock on the door. I don't know why I didn't wake him up. I think I thought I was dreaming. I walk down the stairs slowly, I hear someone call my name and it sounds like Lilly. With the sound of the storm muffling her voice it sounds like Lilly was on the other side of the world. I wasn't expecting her to be here because she started school weeks ago – again I think it's all a dream. I get closer to the door and look through the peep hole. I stand back quickly and puzzled, it was Lilly what the hell was she doing here? I open the door and she was a panicked wet mess. She was supposed to be at college a couple of weeks ago. I let her inside the house and she collapses on the floor crying. Lilly's shirt was completely torn open and her bra was torn as well. Her right eye was completely swollen and her lip was busted, she had been beaten.

"Lilly, what the hell happen to you? Did someone rob you? Kiowa! Ki!" I scream frantically. Kiowa run down the stairs quickly.

"Aquila, Joseph hit me over the head with a lamp. I was over his apartment. We had just got done with a movie. I was raining so I wanted to wait a little for it to die down before leaving to go back to my room. I sit on the couch and then he gives me a bottle of water to drink. After a while the next thing I know I start getting sleepy. I know I had only took about two or three sips. The next thing I know Joseph starts to climb on top of me. I told him to stop! I pushed him off me! But he starts to get more aggressive with me.

"He then started unbuckling my pants. I told him I didn't want to have sex. I got up and went towards the door to leave. Once I got to the door to open it he started beating me. Joseph got my pants off and after that I must have passed out. But then I came back to consciousness and he was on top of me. Aquila, he raped me! I walked in the rain all the way here. What did I do wrong Aquila?" She screams and cries in agony.

"Lilly, I'm so sorry this happened to you. We need to get you to a hospital! You need to get a rape kit done. I will be alright with you the entire way, but you need to get a kit done." I held her face.

"No Aquila! I'm not going to be labeled a whore. If I go then everyone will think I'm some slut who was asking for it to happen. I came over here so Kiowa's mom could fix my face and make sure nothing was broken. I can't go to the hospital!" She screams.

"Look at me! Lilly, look at me! At no point was this is your fault. At no point were you asking to be raped! Do you understand me? Lilly, you are not a whore and even if you were you didn't ask for it. There is not a woman on this earth who was raped and asked for it. There is nothing in the world that can make it OK for a guy to rape a woman. I don't care if you were walking around naked, he should have never done that to you. I'm taking you to the hospital, we can't sit on this!" I try to calm her down.

"No! I can't it hurts too much. I'm nothing but a failure. I dropped out of college before I even went. I deserve bad things. They are going to say I willingly took the drugs." She cries.

"Drugs? Wait… listen to me the night of your party I was drugged too. After I left I started feeling sleepy while I was driving and had to pull over. I almost was in another car accident. Once I got to the hospital I found out that ENT was in my system. Do you think Joseph had anything to do with that? " I ask her calmly.

Lilly just looked at me completely embarrassed. "Really, Quil? Oh my, God. I knew they were into drugs but I didn't know they drugged you too. That's what Joseph and his friends do. They put drugs in people's bottles when they're not looking. It's their way of getting people to loosen up. He has been trying to get me to have sex with him for months now, but I didn't want to do it. I guess tonight he was tired of waiting. I should have stopped talking to him a long time ago. I'm so sorry, Quil. Ok. I'll go to the hospital." She cries.

I saw the most positive person I've known be broken down to nothing. There is nothing worst in being in a situation like this and be helpless. I went to my room and got her some sweats of mine. I sat with her in the back seat of the car and help her while Kiowa drives to the hospital. I held her as tight as I could, whatever I says to get her to agree to get a rape kit I'm glad. No women should ever have to deal with this kind of pain alone. No man should ever think that raping a woman is OK.

Lilly gets the rape kit done. The officers went to question Joseph back at his apartment. Lilly was lifeless as if she was a dead body – I was hurting to see my friend like that. I stayed with her letting her know that it was the right thing to do. She called her mom. I can't even begin to imagine what her mother was feeling. I wish I could take her tears away from her. Once her mother got to the hospital she told me to go home and that she had it from there. I found Ki waiting on me in the waiting room. Even though we all are friends, I told Kiowa it wouldn't be a good idea for him to be around her. We went home and attempted to sleep. The next morning Lilly texted me telling me the DNA test of course was a match to him and he was arrested on a rape and drug charge.

I went to see Lilly every day following her rape, she was doing better. The physical scars were healing, but the emotional ones were still open. Joseph was charged with sexual assault with a controlled substance and assault with a deadly weapon. I know Lilly will never be the same, but it's good to see that she working to get better. She's still trying to keep her positive outlook on life which is helping her heal. Time around her family is good for her. She needs to be around loving people that care about her. She may never be able to fully trust a man again, but at least she's healing.

After all that has gone down over the last few weeks my birthday rolls around and I'm depressed just like every year. There just something about the whole idea of celebrating your birth that doesn't get me in a happy mood. However, I have been working hard to run the store every day since its opening. I decide if I am to do anything to celebrate my birth, I'm going to take the day off and do nothing. The best thing in the world for me was to be able to relax.

It was a perfect October seventeenth; the weather was warm considering we were entering fall. Kiowa had left a surprise birthday breakfast for me with a cute card with a cat on it. I had the whole house to myself for a couple of hours. All day long I sat on the couch watching bad reality TV. I was by myself enjoying a little well-deserved me time. I had lived a hard eighteen years, my goal is to make year nineteen an even better year – it was time to break the cycle of being depressed. I sat on the porch and watch the sunset. I was wearing a green sweater with grey sweat pants and house shoes. The leaves were starting to fall and change color. It was a nice way to finish up my evening.

Kiowa came home right when I was walking in the house. He had balloons and flowers for me. He told me he had plans for us and that I should go upstairs and put on something nice. I really wanted to stay home, but I go upstairs and got change and go along with what Ki wanted to do. He blind folded me, which I hated and it made me nervous, but I trust Ki. He walks me to the car and starts to drive. The thing about being blind folded in a car is you feel everything. There were so many twists and turns I thought I was going to throw up all over the place.

Kiowa stops the car and I almost fall over in the front seat because I wasn't expecting to the stop. I'm not the most coordinated person in the world. I always fall over air, if my life turned into a horror movie then I will be the first to die. As he helps me out he car I almost trip again, but Ki catches me before I tumble into the dirt. It was quiet the only thing I could hear was crickets. Kiowa spends me around a couple of times. He untied the blind fold, when he did that Koda started setting off fireworks. Ms. Maddox had a cake made for me. She had made so much food it could feed an entire army. I don't think she knows how to make a meal for just four people.

"Kiowa, you didn't need to go through all of this trouble for me. None of you did. Thank you, I appreciate it!" I smile and start to hug everyone.

"None sense, my dear. I love you like a daughter. This was nothing compared to what I really wanted to do." She hugs me as hard as she could.

"I'm just so happy, I got to blow something up." Koda laughs.

"Quil, this is your first birthday without your parents being here. I know that every year you get depressed as it is, but I want to start year nineteen off with joy." Ki holds me in his arms.

"Kiss me." I smile.

Kiowa and Koda were wrestling for a while. While the boys were busy trying to kill each other, Ms. Maddox and I played checkers. Koda still tries to mess with Kiowa forgetting that his older brother was captain of the wrestling team. Ms. Maddox looks at her sons and with only a look a mother could give to make them stop. Over all I had a pretty good day. We hang out for a little while longer and then we all head back to our homes.

I look up at the stars while Kiowa drives us home. I didn't say anything, but in my head I was holding a conversation with God. There is not enough praise I could give him. I could have died along with my parents that night and not have lived to see another year. I do admit I don't like the fighting, but before things went left in their relationship everything was normal. I turn my head and watch Kiowa as he drives the car. It still amazes me that I'm in love with my best friend. He didn't notice that I was staring at him like he was a deer while I hunt him.

Once we were home I get out of the car and went into the house. Kiowa was bringing the gifts from his mother into the house. I never officially welcomed Kiowa to the home. While he was bringing in the presents I slip upstairs to the room. I'm not used to having to hide something from someone in the house. The night set that I bought from Feather's was perfectly hidden folded between one of my shirts. I quickly changed clothes and went downstairs as he was bringing in the last of my gifts. There was a nervous feeling that I was unable to shake. Kiowa turned around and saw me in the short, see-though gown with the push up bra and a thong. He accidently dropped the gifts, not once did he take his eyes off me. Personally I think he was trying to figure out where to look first. He stood still not knowing what to say. I watch his eyes follow me around as I came down the stairs.

"So are you going to say something?" I laugh at him as I am walking down the stairs.

"You look…wow…" He couldn't talk.

"Come on let's head upstairs." I smile and place my hand on his face.

"Quil?" He pulls my hands away from his face.

"What?" I try to kiss him, but he stops me.

"That night on the beach I didn't want to take it that far. I planned for that to happen on our wedding night. I let my hormones take over my mind, but I guess it doesn't matter since we are getting married. This is going to be our last time doing this before the wedding." He looks at me while holding my hands.

"Since it's our last, let's make it our best." I says smiling. I grab his hand guiding him upstairs to our room.

Restless One

Today marks one year since the death of my parents. In one year so much has changed for me in so little time. I thought that today I would be depressed, but I'm not. I'm the complete opposite, today I seem to be normal. There nothing wrong with me other than feeling sick. I must be coming down with the flu or getting some type of cold. I can't seem to keep anything down. I think it's just my nerves getting to me, Kiowa thinks it's the flu. Whatever is going wrong with my body I gladly would like it to stop. I jump out of bed and dress myself in sweats. I wait for Kiowa downstairs. He wants to take me to work today, I believe he thinks I'm going to have a nervous breakdown or something. If I do it, it wouldn't be the first time.

I should have closed the store today. Almost every single person who has come into Waters has says, "Sorry for your loss.", as if I need to be reminded. And even though I'm not feeling sad, I'm wondering if people realizing it's the anniversary of their deaths will send me into a sad mood. I want to forget about the accident as much as possible. Although they're gone, they will never be forgotten. And I want to be strong today. I'm not perfect and I'm not trying to be, but I just don't want to be sad today. The last twelve months I have gone through a lot of changes, in my eyes there's not a lot that still needs fixing with me. I'm good, I'm OK, and I'm at peace.

The day didn't turn out that bad. I was finally at my favorite part of my day - closing time. There was a significant amount of shoppers today, mainly because of the anniversary of my parents' death. Waters was completely ruined, but in a good way. The store was a mess from the shoppers. Luckily for me, I had a burst of energy to be able to get the store cleaned before leaving for the day. I swept, mopped and dusted the entire store. After examining the store and the inventory it seems that everyone bought junk food today. The shelves that were stocked with chips were almost empty, I was wondering if today was national chip day or something. I mean I was so busy today I didn't even see that the shelves were half way empty. I start crying and I couldn't understand why I was crying. I was an emotional hormonal mess. I mean come on, it was only an empty chip rack. I put my back toward the shelf and slide down onto the floor. I sat on the half wet floor for no reason just crying. It made absolutely no sense to me why I was so emotion. Maybe I was finally succumbing to the thoughts of my parents not being around. Eventually I got off the floor and stop myself from crying. I continue with restocking like any other day.

I wait in the back office for Kiowa to get here to pick me up. Once he arrived I was so tired I just want to go home and relax. He didn't question me either, he said I look like a walking skeleton. When we got home I just went upstairs and hop in my bed without showering or anything.

Ki comes in with something for me to eat. "Hey, I made you a small bowl of soup with a turkey sandwich." He says as he comes and sits on the bed and hands me the tray of food.

"Thanks, I'm not hungry. I just don't feel good right now, my stomach is so upset. I'm going to go ahead to sleep. Ki, I don't want you to think that I'm upset about the anniversary. After a year I'm fine with their passing." I say looking down at the tray of food.

"Ok, but if at any time you feel yourself getting depressed, please let me know. I'm going to put this in the fridge in case you get hungry later." He kisses my forehead were my scars are located.

"Kiowa, why do you always kiss my scars? You never kiss the other side. I ask you that at Sal's a couple of months ago when I first opened the store again. You always dance around that question when I ask." I question him.

"What scars? I only see a tree." He looks at me with a straight face.

"Tree?" I was confused. Not something good being compared to a piece of wood.

"Think about it, Quil. Your face resembles that of a tree. There are thousands of trees on this earth, not one is alike. Baby, your scars are that of a unique tree. Aquila, you're one of a kind. The earth wouldn't be able to survive without trees. Just like how I can't live without you, just like the earth can't survive with trees. Aquila, you are the most important thing in the world to me. I love you for what's in your heart and in your mind. I loved you before the accident and I'm madly in love you now. When we go out together I see people looking at us and I know you notice as well. I want them to look at the true face of beauty." Kiowa kisses my forehead again and proceeds to walk out the room. There are just some things you can't change about a person, and hat part of Ki I never want to change. I turn over and go to sleep.

That next day Koda comes over to visit us. He had a huge paper that was due next week, I don't know why he decided to wait until the last moment to do it. I made him do an outline of all the topics that he needs to put into the paper. He just wanted to do the paper and get it over with, not understanding that in a paper based on history he needed to be as thorough as possible. There is a lot of important facts that goes into a history paper, it's not a paper you can just throw together. He sat there complaining about everything I was telling him to do. I yell at him to make him quit bitching about something he had three weeks to do. I was still not feeling well and all I could think about is why I couldn't shake this cold. I didn't want to be bothered with Koda. I was so pissed he knew that I was sick but begged me help him. I just wanted to sleep.

We worked on the paper all day and I lost track of time, when I looked up day was turning into night. He still was nowhere near being complete with the paper. I told him that he had a good start and should be able to finish the rest of the paper on his own. My body was slowly giving out, I was so drained I didn't even know what to do. I told Koda that it was time for him to leave and just spent the rest of the time sitting on the couch feeling miserable.

Later that evening, Kiowa ends up waking me up to see if I was OK. I look over at the TV clock it was three-thirty in the morning. I slept the entire evening away. He brought me tomato soup, which is my favorite soup in the world. Kiowa hands me the bowl of warm soup. The smell of the soup had completely made me nauseous. I couldn't run to the bathroom fast enough to vomit, there was no food on my stomach to throw up. I felt like my whole stomach was going to come out of my body. My head was hurting so bad it could have exploded. If I am to die let me not go like this, a freaking mess. This was the first time in my entire life I thought my stomach was going to come out of my throat.

No one on this earth looks good while vomiting their brains out. Kiowa came to the bathroom and stood in the door way. I told him to not look at me and to go away, this was kind of embarrassing, well for me anyway. He walks over to me sits on the side of the tub, rubbing my back trying to help me. I had just woken up from my sleep, yet I was still so tired. Kiowa gets up from the tub and goes over to the towel rack, wetting a towel, and putting it on the back of my neck. He braids my hair so that I wouldn't get any vomit on it. Not too soon after that, the vomiting seems to have stopped. Kiowa managed to pick me up, carrying me up the stairs, and into the bedroom. He places me on to the bed, pulled the covers on top of me, and rubs my forehead while holding me. We spend the rest of the morning just watching TV.

"Aquila, you need to go to the doctor if this continues on." Kiowa says while rubbing my head.

"Kiowa it's just a cold, you know my body hates me some times. It has always taken me longer to get over the flu. It took me two months to get over the common cold last year." I say weakly.

"Ok, if it doesn't get better soon, then I'm alerting the Sargent." He laughs.

"There is no need for you to alert your mother. I'm fine, it's just a cold." I say half asleep.

When I'm sick I love being at home in my bed sleeping, but I'm not a teenager anymore. I can't, it would be nice if I was able to. I'm starting to get better, which is good. Ms. Maddox is trying to keep up with my family tradition, lately she has been inviting us over on Wednesday for dinner. This also gives her a chance to see her son, she lies saying she doesn't miss him. Koda told me a day or two after Kiowa moved Ms. Maddox went into his room with a stool and just cried. Her birds nest is missing one of her chicks. I know she's happy that her son is happy, but she only has Kiowa and Koda.

Ms. Maddox house feels so much like home for me. There is a lot of history in her home for me. I can't tell you how many times I have injured myself from chasing Kiowa and Koda around. It was kind of like my home away from home. My escape if you will. I'm not that much excited about the wedding, but she is.

"Aquila, you and I should start looking at wedding dresses! You're going to be a beautiful bride, well you're already so gorgeous." Ms. Maddox excitement grew the more she talks about the wedding.

"Sure, Ms. Maddox, we can start looking." I say nervously.

"Come on I have some books we could look at right now. You would look stunning in a long sleeve dress. We must go dress shopping one day soon. I'm so proud of you both, who would have thought one day you two would be married?" She grabs my hand, taking me to her room to look at magazines, leaving Koda and Kiowa to themselves.

"I'm only going to say this once Kiowa. This is a rare brother to brother moment, you're one lucky guy. How did you find the perfect women this young? Aquila is smart, funny, and talent. Don't hit me but she's hot too - before and after the accident. Not bad big brother!" Koda puts his left arm around Kiowa's neck.

"I don't know, but I'm glad I did. I'm truly lucky to look at that red diamond every day." Kiowa smiles.

"What's a red diamond? Diamonds are all clear." Koda ask looking at Kiowa like he was stupid.

"A red diamond is the most expensive diamond in the world. It's extremely rare. A single carat can go for millions of dollars. Aquila is that rare red diamond." Kiowa smiles looking at

the house.

A Spring from the Base of a Mountain

Today I woke up feeling brand new, the sun was shining and I was feeling like my body had finally gotten rid of the flu. Waters was also unusually busy this morning which was weird. It was a quarter to noon, one of my customers told me that the feminine hygiene aisle was missing tampons. I told her we have some in the back. I left the counter and went into the back stock room to get some. I grab the stool to fill the basket up with them to take them into the store, once again being short doesn't help me. I stood on my toes reaching for them and I fell knocking them off the shelf. One of the boxes of tampons hits me in the head. While picking them off the floor I realized I couldn't remember the last time I got my period.

My entire body went cold, all the blood rushed too my feet. Since the accident my cycle tends to skip. Normally when my period would be late, I just understood that it was going to be a day or two over. Considering how my period has been skipping since the accident, and well me and Kiowa have been you know, I might be pregnant. I know that I and Kiowa are going to be married soon, but a baby. This completely changes everything. I tried to remain as calm as possible.

I walk out of the stock room like nothing ever even happen. I continue throughout the day like there was nothing going on. In the back of my mind I couldn't get out the possibility that there could be a baby growing inside of me. Once there was a break and no one was in the store I lock up the store. I quickly ran to the feminine aisle and grab a home pregnancy test. I was scared, but it was a good scared. I must point out that peeing on that tiny stick was that hardest thing I have ever had to do. My stomach was in a knot, waiting to see if I was pregnant felt like an eternity. I felt like the rest of my life was going be decided in fifteen minutes.

I paced in the bathroom back and forth waiting to see what the future had store for us. Fifteen long minutes later, the tiny stick reveals two pink lines, I'm pregnant. The knot that was in my stomach began to loosen up. Hell, the entire time I thought I just had the flu. I guess I'll have the flu for next nine months.

I stare at that stick for a minute, there were too many emotions for me to be able to process everything at once. There was soon to be a person growing inside of me. The tears I cried were of joy and nervousness. I had to calm myself down, I need a doctor to confirm this. I can't go to Ms. Maddox otherwise she will start buying baby clothes before we even know what we are having. A baby, I couldn't get the thought of it out of my head. I walked out of the bathroom with the biggest smile on my face. It quickly went away, Kiowa was outside of the door waiting for me and wondering why I closed it up so soon. It's too early for him to know, not only that but I'm not sure if it's true.

I walk over to the door trying to keep my composure, the smile on my face wouldn't die.

"Are you closing up shop early today?" He shrugs.

"No. Someone knocked over a jar of jam. I had to mop the floor." I lie to him with a straight face.

"Well for someone who just had to clean up jam you're sure in a good mood. I take it you are feeling much better?" He hugs me.

"Yeah, I feel much better now." I say flipping over the sign from closed to open.

This is truly a huge blessing from God. Kiowa looks at me as if he knows something was up. This was hard trying to play off, I just want to burst out tell him I'm pregnant. He stays with me for a minute just checking on me, you know being a good future husband.

Luckily I was able find a doctor on the other side of Ruben. I couldn't risk running into Ms. Maddox, even though the only thing I want to do is tell everyone. The Ob-Gyn I'm seeing is part of Days Hospital and it was packed full of women who look like they were ready to give birth at that very seconded. I sit there for an hour waiting to be called in. Everyone in there probably thought I was a creep. I examined all those women up in there, the joy was replaced with fear.

The nurse calls me back the examination room, the more questions she ask the more nervous I got. I met with the doctor who explained the changes my body will be making. Dr. Barker had to be no older than twenty-six years old, long black hair that was tied up into a ponytail. She wanted to do a blood test to confirm my pregnancy. Dr. Barker was a vampire, she took five tubes of blood out of me. Once she was done draining the blood form my body that was it. I would hear the verdict in the next week or two. In my opinion waiting a week to find out you're pregnant is torture. I think I am but who knows my body could be playing a trick on me. I went home slightly disappointed, but happy and nervous at the same time. The next thing I'm concerned about is how am I going to tell Kiowa about the baby if I am pregnant? I have to figure something out, sadly I can't just wait till my belly pops out and say, *oh yeah, by the way...* His birthday is coming up, I'll try to hold it in till them maybe.

That night I look at myself in the mirror trying to picture myself with a huge belly. I'm not a skinny girl, but a baby, wow. I was looking in the mirror so hard I didn't even notice Kiowa in the background staring at me. He walks up to me and hugs me from behind. It's funny he has no idea that our lives are about to change again. I like not being able to tell him about the baby. It's my special little secret.

"So, what are you staring at other than that beautiful face of yours?" He smiles at me.

"Nothing! I just was picturing the wedding day." I smile and turn around to look at him.

"Well I didn't expect you to be so happy about the wedding. Has someone kidnapped my fiancé and replaced her with the same beautiful girl. What changed your mind?" He laughs while hugging me.

"Yeah, things change. I don't know what changed my mind. I just have been thinking about it a lot more lately. I'm happy to know that I will be becoming you wife that's all." I smile playing it off. Trying to keep the biggest secret of your life to yourself is hard. Not to mention having to wait to hear back from the doctor's office.

It's been a couple of days and waiting to hear back from the doctor is killing me. A part of me still wonders how I didn't notice my period not coming went on for so long. My body always disobeys what it's supposed to do. This is the only time that I'm happy that it didn't listen to me. It was ten-thirty in the morning, I was working the counter and didn't hear the phone ring. I had missed the call from the hospital, the nurse left a voice mail. I listen to the voice mail and am elated to discover that I'm thirteen weeks pregnant. This makes me two months since my birthday was a little over two months ago. The nurse gave me some instructions and foods to stay away from. Although there is going to be a lot of research that I must do on my part. Luckily Waters sells prenatal vitamins so I can start of there.

I have no idea where the road in front of me is going to take me. I'm a little bit scared and nervous about what could now happen. Whatever happens I will take it all in good spirits. It's funny the thought of me becoming a mom. I don't care if I have a son or a daughter, I will love them no matter what. If I'm carrying a daughter there is so much I have to teacher her. I mean come on, girls can be a lot to deal with sometimes. Kiowa has no choice but to deal with me once I finally tell him. If I'm carrying a boy, I will have no idea what I'm doing. I have lived my whole nineteen years as a girl. I'm going to enjoy the next couple of months. I am a woman, I was made for this. Woman are like trees, we are able to grow and create life from inside of us.

Eternal Blossom

I am a house

I am a house that was broken in.

I am a house that was abuse and misconstrued

Broken windows, holes in the walls

The house screams begging someone to save it

I am the house no one wants.

There was a man who saw beauty in the house

The man rebuilds the house making it a home again

Sixteen-weeks pregnant my clothes are starting not to fit me anymore, even though I live in sweats on a daily they are not fitting perfectly. I'm hoping Kiowa and everyone else just thinks I've gained weight. Although I don't believe he has noticed anything. I can tell the baby is going to get me in trouble, the smell of food is killing me. Morning sickness is the worst thing that has happened to me so far. Along with my body being sore all the time the only thing I want is a long bath with a back rub, being pregnant is hard – keeping it a secret is harder.

Kiowa's birthday is this week and I can't hold the secret in any longer. He told his mom that a small family dinner would be perfect along with her famous chocolate cake. I have tried to come up with the most fantastic baby reveal. Sadly, *there's no you knock me up* shirt that I can run out and buy on short notice. There are about fifty things running through my brain right now. This is going to affect us for this rest of our lives and his or her life.

It's weird shopping in the baby section, but also exciting. I think God is going to give me a boy. I believe this because the first man that was ever supposed to love me didn't or he didn't know the correct way of showing it. Now I'm not saying that my dad was a bad guy all the time, his father skipped out on him and my grandmother before he was born – so he didn't know any better. My mom used to always say the reason we didn't get along was because we were the same. If my dad were still alive I would have given him another chance, even though it would be chance number seven thousand. All I could have done is hoped for things to get better. I will be seeing myself through the eyes of a parent and not a normal teenager.

I walk up and down each aisle of the baby section, I have no idea how I'm going to tell him. Do I go with a onesie? Or baby bottle? There was a blue pacifier right next to a toy for babies when they start teething. In my life, sometimes you just know when things are perfect. The pacifier was the perfect way for me to tell him about the baby. I bought a medium size black box, white ribbon, blue tissue paper. I might not be able to go all out like he did for me, but I think it's perfect nonetheless. Now the only problem I have is where to hide it. I can't hide it in the house with the fear of him finding out before his birthday. The only place I think he won't be able to find it is in my car. Hopefully he would be needing to use it the next couple of days.

I'm praying Kiowa won't find out about the baby until his birthday. Ms. Maddox planned a birthday dinner for him and invited some of his friends. The whole day I was helping Kiowa's mom set up for the part. I don't understand how she works more than forty hours a week and still has this much energy. I work all day, every day and am extremely tired at the end of each day. Ms. Maddox is definitely a super hero, she is truly amazing. I have said it before and I will say it again. Ms. Maddox still sees her sons as her babies, her favorite thing to do is completely embarrass them as much as possible. During Ki's party she keeps killing on him and hugging him and making everyone sing happy birthday to him. I was embarrassed for him because Ms. Maddox was absolutely doing the most.

After a good evening of festivities all of Kiowa's friends came together to give him one final birthday wish and they all left at the same time. It was just the four of us left, I figured it was the perfect time to tell Ki the baby. I went to the trunk of the car and got the box out the car.

"I didn't get a chance to give you my gift yet. It's not much, but I hope you like it." I was smiling nervously. I walk over to him standing by the logs Ms. Maddox uses as seats. I walk away from Kiowa and sat on the log opposite of everyone.

"It's from you, Quil. Of course he would like it regardless of what's in there. There can be nothing in there and he will still be happy." Koda laughs.

"Koda be nice to your brother. Go ahead, son, open your gift." Ms. Maddox says looking at Koda then turning her head to look at Kiowa.

The moment of truth he starts to undo the ribbon. My stomach was in such a knot I thought I was going to shit myself. He had a normal straight look on his face. He removes the top off the box. The pacifier was sitting on top of the blue tissue paper. He looks at me and reads the words on the pacifier 'Mommy's Baby'.

"Mommy's Baby?!" Koda fell of the log laughing. "Quil, that's a good one."

"Mommy's baby? You think I'm still a baby. Sorry to disappoint you, Quil. I won't be able to use this." He laughs while everything went right over his head."

"Wait a minute?" Ms. Maddox looks as if she figured out the secret. She then looks over at me.

"Well, it's not for you. It's for the baby." I say messing with my hands.

"Baby?" He pauses in shock.

"I'm pregnant, Kiowa. You're going to be a dad." I say to him wide eyed and smiling, waiting for his response.

"Aquila, baby, your pregnant?!" He drops everything running over to me.

"Yeah, a baby, Kiowa." I smile.

"I'm going to be a grandmother? I can't believe this! How far along are you?" Ms. Maddox asks as she was practically jumping up and down.

"I'm thirteen weeks." I respond.

"You make me so happy you don't even know it! The love of my life is creating life!!" He says kissing me, picking me up, and swinging me around.

Koda looks like he was in shock while their mom starts to cry. I have never been happier than in this moment with my family. I don't think I have ever seen a smile that big on Kiowa's face before. The entire ride home all Kiowa could talk about was the baby and was touching my stomach. There's a lot that needs to be done around the house before the baby gets here. The two of us are becoming three.

As I settle into my pregnancy I realize that I would take back pain over morning sickness any day. Vomiting every single day is taking the life out of me. It's beautiful to know that I am

creating life from the inside out. Still every morning my insides

seem to be coming out of me. I'm in the bathroom vomiting my

brains out and I feel like I have a hangover every single day

without the drinking. Kiowa hears me vomiting from upstairs and

comes to bathroom. I was so upset I started to cry my eyes out, the

reason for me crying don't ask me. I have no idea why I start

crying, I just think I want the morning sickness to go away. He

comes and tries to comfort me by rubbing my back

"Kiowa, go away leave me to die." I say in between

vomiting.

"Quil, the least I can do is massage your back. You have

just given up your body for us to carry our baby. It would be

selfish of me not to come in here and care. Even though I'm not

the one carrying our child doesn't mean I won't help you." He says

while rubbing my back.

I need to go shopping for new clothes, my other clothes are

starting to not to fit anymore. I'm just going to stick to sweat pants

and t-shirts they don't cost that much. Plus it's much easier to buy.

My days are starting to get shorter. It's every day when I go to open Waters the moment I stick the key into the door, I'm closing and getting ready to go home. Pretty soon my child will be here before I know it.

I close Waters for the day and head for home. All I could think about was getting into bed, shutting my eyes, and going to sleep. I have been so side tracked lately that I haven't had a chance to be able to get my car fixed. My brakes are starting to squeak every time I step on them it sounds like I'm killing two cats. At some point I must set out time to go to Vicks to get them looked at. Kiowa fixes me a plate of leftovers from two nights ago. We ate dinner and sat on the couch watching a horror movie. I was so tired I fall asleep, I assume Kiowa carried me up to the room because the next morning I woke up in the bed.

It's the weekend, Ms. Maddox invited us over to her house. She says she has a surprise for us. Knowing Ms. Maddox who knows what the hell she has planned for us. The outside of the house looks completely normal, as soon as we pulled up she comes rushing outside to greet us. She pulls my hand walking inside the house. Ms. Maddox went shopping and bought a changing table, crib, car seat, and a stroller. She will be the crazy grandmother

who will spoil her grandchild. Luckily, we came over in the truck

otherwise he would have to come back to collect everything. My

baby bump has already started to show, honestly, I just look like I

have put on an extra twenty pounds. She forces us to stay and have

lunch with her. All she could talk about was the baby. She also

starts to describe what giving birth is going to be like. If I could

have jumped out the window unharmed I would have. Kiowa told

her that the first ultra sound was coming up, I want to hit him in his

chest. Her excitement is starting to be a bit much for me, I'm

nervous about the whole pregnancy thing and I'm sure she'll be

hounding me that day about what is seen on the ultrasound.

The next day I finally get a chance to get my car checked

on. My damn car is driving me insane, before I head to Waters

today I'm going to Vicks. Vick's was owned by an older man who

hates mass produced auto repairs shops. Victor reminds me of my

grandfather, he could fix anything it didn't matter how big or small

it was. Victor had to be in his eighties. He still gets up and comes

to work every day. Vicks has been open fifty years and it doesn't

look like Victor is getting ready to retire anytime soon. One thing I like about Vicks, it feels like family. I got there right before they open, the door has a bell attached to the top so that they can hear when someone comes in. The younger guy behind the counter name was Isaac, according to his name tag, he takes my keys and writes down my information.

I sit in the waiting room for an hour, Isaac come and tell me my car is ready. I paid for the service and I go to the big door standing waiting for one of the guys to pull it out. My back was facing the door when the unexpected happened.

"Hey, Aquila!" Taika says with a smile.

Taika pops out of my car surprisingly. Apparently he was the one working on my brakes. If I would have known that he works here I would have definitely went on another side of town to get my car fixed. I can't seem to get away from him – after all this time I thought he was finally out of our lives. I haven't seen him in a couple months since he came to my house apologizing to me. Even though we have moved pass everything being next to him is still awkward. He held my keys in his hand which forces me to have a conversation with him.

"Hey, Taika." I say awkwardly looking for my quickest escape.

"So, long time no see. What you been up to?" He smiles.

"You know, nothing much just working at the shop." I respond staring at my keys in his hand.

"Yeah, I've been here the last couple months. I have been taking care of Ayanna since my mom OD'd last month. It pays good, so I'm here making the best of things." He says with a somber, yet nonchalant tone.

"Sorry for your loss." I took a pause. It's kind of weird asking for you key back when someone tells you their mother has died.

"You look good! Things still going good with Kiowa?" He says with a curious tone.

"Yeah we are still together. Can I get my keys?" I say with quickness. I was done with the conversation when he brought up Ki.

"Hey, Aquila, I'm sorry. I just always think there is hope for me to make it right with you for real." He says while handing me the keys to my car.

"Taika, I'm sorry, but there is nothing that will happen with us you blew it. I have a lot going with the wedding and the baby…" I didn't mean to tell him about the baby it just came out so naturally.

"You're pregnant?" He says with a sad voice.

"Yes, I got to go." I say and quickly grab my keys and rush out. I try to get the door of my car open but Taika rushes after me and grab my wrist and wouldn't let go of me. I told him to let go of me before I scream.

"Aquila, I want you to listen to me for a minute. I'm sorry just please listen to me. I love you." He looks at me dead in my eyes.

"Taika, let me go!" I say scared.

I slam the door of my car as quick as I can and drive off. What Taika says to me doesn't make any sense what so ever. He loves me? I realize that I didn't have the keys to the store. I hate that I had to go all the way back home to get them. Kiowa was leaving out for work when I get there. I guess he must up have picked up on the energy that I was upset. A normal life is something that I would like to have for once. I told him what happen and that Taika grab me. I probably should not have told Ki that but I was still in the moment. Ki was upset, but was more concerned about me than anything. I got the keys to Waters and head for work. The whole way there I keep thinking about what he said. Why can't Taika get over me?

After the fiasco with Taika, I was so excited for the next day. It was Wednesday I finally get to see my baby for the first time ever. Ms. Maddox says that if she wasn't in surgery she would stop just so she can see as well… unfortunately for me she didn't have surgery. The nurse Tiffany asks me a thousand questions then instructs me to lie on my back. Tiffany applies this cold gel on my stomach, then takes this takes this thing that looks like something from space and pushes it on my stomach. She looks around for a minute without saying anything. I'm holding Kiowa's hand the entire time. She turns on the screen, almost instantly the blood leaves my body rushing to my feet. There was this thing that looked like any alien that was my child. The room was dead silent until we saw the baby. The baby looks like a bobble head doll almost. I have never known such happiness in my entire life. It's a feeling that I can't explain, it's a feeling only mothers would know.

"Looks like you're going to have a summer baby. Your baby is going to be here sometime in June. Would you like to know the sex?" Tiffany asks.

"Yes!" I say nervously squeezing Kiowa's hand tighter.

"Look at the screen." She says, pressing buttons.

The screen was blank with only our baby on it. The nurse counted down, then it pops up on the screen.

"Congrats, you're having a girl! And now for her heart beat." Tiffany smiles.

"Yes!" Ms. Maddox screams.

"I'm so happy." Kiowa says looking at the screen.

I start to cry. Kiowa kisses my forehead. Hearing her heartbeat was amazing. It makes it all so real for me, there truly is life growing inside of me. There's this tiny thing forming skin and bones each second of the day. Luckily Ms. Maddox works in this hospital, otherwise they would have put her out for screaming. I thought it was going to be a boy, but I would have been happy with whatever. All I really want is a healthy baby with ten fingers and ten toes. Tiffany cleans the gel off my belly, Kiowa helps me off the table. She gives me a couple copies of the ultrasound pictures. Kiowa's favorite thing to do now is to rub my belly and talk to the baby. Kiowa and I leave the hospital and he drives me to the store. Nothing could possible ruin this perfect Wednesday.

"I guess now that we know it's a girl we can start looking at names." Kiowa laughs glancing at me.

"Whatever her name will be it will come to us. 'Till then we can just call her *bobbles*." I say while looking at him with a big smile.

"Why *bobbles*?" He asks.

"In the ultrasound, her head looks like a bobble head doll." I laugh.

I'm going to need to hire someone to help with the store now that there's a baby involved. I put of a "help wanted" sign in the window. It will take a while before I can find someone, the sooner I find someone the better though. The day went on as normal. Lilly even surprises me today by coming into the store. She looks a lot better and heathier. I just announced that I was pregnant to Kiowa I really haven't had the time to tell her about it. Lilly being Lilly freaks out at the news. She starts going on about how she so excited to be an aunt. Her visit was short, she explains that she needs to head over to the doctors to get checked up. I like that she back to her positive bubbly self.

Kiowa comes to pick me up and we go home. I have been on my feet all day, it was nice that Kiowa helps me take my shoes off and rubs my feet. I wash up and get ready for bed. Kiowa wants to clean up the house, his Mother was kind of going a bit over board with shopping - I head to bed alone.

Being pregnant takes a toll on the body. Of course everyone knows that you have to pee a lot when you're pregnant. For the tenth time that evening I get up to go to the bathroom. It was three in the morning and Kiowa's side of the bed didn't even look touched. I went to the bathroom and started to head downstairs to see where he was at. As I slowly walk down the stairs I could hear people talking. I stopped half-way down and listen in.

"Aquila went to get her breaks fixed. Taika worked on her car, she didn't even know. He found out about the baby. He's upset about that and can't seem to get over himself not being with her. I don't think that this is going to end well." Kiowa says.

"What did the elders say?" Koda asks.

"No one wants to go to war unless they have to. They tried talking to the Nita Tribe Elders, but they consider Taika like their son. I think we're going to be in for a fight. Look, Taika can't seem to get over Quil for some reason, the guy has lost his mind. From what I'm hearing they think that the baby is his and not mine. There swearing that I took Aquila from him. They have created this messed up lie." Kiowa says.

"Son, this could potentially get ugly really quickly. We need to keep Aquila away from anyone who is Nita. All Nita men are marked with a bear on the right side of their chest. I highly doubt they would send any women to do their dirty work. If Taika can lie about this who knows what else could happen. They could try to attack her. We need to keep her safe." Ms. Maddox says.

"Kiowa, if you need anything just ask." Joe says.

"Yeah, you know we have your back through anything. If you need us to help you protect Aquila just ask. Kiowa you would do the same for us if we needed it." Casey says.

"Thanks all of you! I really appreciate it. None of you can tell Aquila about any of this. She's pregnant and I don't want to put any more stress on her. I just need her to focus on the baby. She needs to think everything is normal. I want her to have a smooth pregnancy. We just need to act like nothing's going on around her. I have to see what the council is going to do or if they're going to get involved." Kiowa says.

My ears couldn't believe what I was hearing. Things were supposed to be normal for once. Why do I always have bullshit in my life? I finish walking down the stairs, tears running down my face - I was hurt.

"Kiowa, I can't believe you lied to me. We are about to have a baby and you hiding all this from me?! How could you not tell me any of this was happening? How could none of you tell me about this?" I ask crying.

"Quil, you weren't supposed to find out." Kiowa shakes his head disappointed that I found out.

Kiowa turns around and looks me in the eyes. I didn't allow him to say anything else to me. I run upstairs locking the door to our bedroom. I lie in bed rubbing my belly. The tears I shed were not for me, they were for my baby whose life I was now not sure of. This is something serious that shouldn't have been hidden from me. I get that he's trying to protect me, but we can no longer be selfish. The decisions we make from now on will affect our child. Kiowa and Ms. Maddox come to the door trying to get me to come out, but I just need time to think. I eventually get up and unlock the door but I kept the door shut. Kiowa comes back later and checks to see if the door was still locked.

He knocks on the door and eases into the room like a mouse looking for food. I just give him the side eye. He had a tray of food in his hand, slowly Kiowa walks toward me. I watch every move he makes as he came toward me. The tray of food contains a turkey sandwich with a bowl of sliced cucumbers covered in salt and pepper. There were so many emotions running through me I didn't know which one was the strongest now. Kiowa got to the end of the bed and sat the tray of food down. I hadn't eaten all day long so I was starting to get hungry. I can tell he didn't want to make eye contact with me, he keeps looking at me and looking at the ground. I would be scared to look me in the eyes if I was him. He was nervous and didn't know how or what to say to me. I look him up and down not saying anything, he didn't know how to face me.

"Thank you for the food." I say giving him a snarling look.

"You're welcome. Look, I'm sorry I didn't tell you. I had no intention in making you upset or worried. I honestly wanted you to move on like none of this was going on." He reaches and rubs my belly.

"What are we going to do?" I say placing my hand on top of his.

"You don't have to worry about anything. I have two women that I need to take care of now. I just want you to relax and let me handle this." Kiowa half smiles at me.

This whole situation started from me, everything that is going on is my fault. Taika knew what he was doing when he saw I brought my car into Vicks that day. I don't know how Bobbles is handling this from the inside, but I'm having a hard time processing this. Kiowa has been going to meet with the council a lot more lately. Some Nita tribe members don't want to hear anything we are trying to say. Every person who comes into the store I'm scared of. I'm terrified someone's going to hurt me or the baby.

There's nothing worse than being afraid. Kiowa's doing his best to try to make everything go as smoothly as possible. When I came home from work Kiowa had a surprise for me. All I just want to do is go to bed and die of depression. He walks me up the staircase holding my hand the entire time. I had no idea that he had turned the study into the nursey in a couple of hours. His mom bought a white crib which he places right in the center of the room. There was a grey fluffy carpet placed under the crib. The changing table was set in the corner far away from the crib. There was a pink elephant Ms. Maddox had swaddle placed inside the crib. There were a couple of girlie things place around the room. I gazed into the crib imagining our baby here and safe in our arms. There was something missing, I left out the room and look for this small box in our closet. My grandmother had made a dream catcher for me when I was young. I went back into the room and placed it at the foot of the crib. Kiowa walks up behind me and wrapped his arms around me. I turned around, look at him, and kiss him. I couldn't ask for anything more.

Twenty weeks pregnant and I'm starting to understand who women really are. My body is starting to do things I never thought would happen a day in my life. I blame everything on the pregnancy right now. I have this strange craving for extremely spicy food. Normally I hate spicy food, but lately I can't seem to get enough of it - the hotter the better. My doctor told me for twenty weeks I'm big. Most people think I'm having twins which I should take as an insult but I don't.

Even with all that's going on I keep trying to push forward. I have to block out that the Nita tribe has been threatening us. They're starting to drive around the house just to keep us on edge. We can only do some much and the council really isn't saying anything to us or trying to help us.

It was midday on a normal day and Waters hasn't been busy as it usually is. I went to stock room to get some supplies when I came out Taika was standing there waiting for me. I instantly got chills up my spine. What makes him think that it's OK to come in here with all the mess he has caused me. I was about to kick him out the store when Joe walked in.

"The hell you doing in here? You have no business being around here and you know that." Joe says.

"This has nothing to do with you. I just need to explain everything to her. Why don't you leave me alone with her?" Taika says pissed.

"You know damn well I'm not going to do that!" Joe says getting in Taika's face.

Joe slams Taika into the one of the shelves full of cleaning supplies. He gets off the floor and then looks Joe in his face and leaves. He checks to see if I was OK, before calling Kiowa to let him know what happened. Everyone, when they are free, stop by to check making sure that the store and I were OK, but there mainly just coming to see me. Kiowa comes shortly after, of course he was worried about me and Bobbles. We close a little early than normal, but after today I really wasn't up for much after Taika showed up. Instead of going home right away I told Kiowa we should go to Sal's and make it a quick date. I didn't want to talk about anything pertaining to our current situation. I wanted to just focus on us and the baby.

We ate and then left heading for home, it had snowed earlier in the day. It looked like someone had thrown glitter all over the place. I like it when the light catches a new batch of snow. God sure does know how to make the land beautiful. Once we get to the house Kiowa helped me out the car. It's hard to move with all the extra weight around. I laugh every time I need help with getting up. We walk up the side walk to the house, as we were walking three cars pull up. Kiowa and I stop, the cars were full of men. There were seven of them and the men look like they lived in the gym. One of the guys had his shirt open and there was a bear tattooed on his chest. They get out of their cars and start walking toward us.

"Hey, Kiowa! We need to talk to you." One of the guys yells out.

"Quil, listen to me go in the house and lock the door. Don't come out no matter what happens! OK?" Kiowa says pushing me behind him.

"Ki?!" I say nervously.

"Aquila, go now!" He says worried about my safety.

I walk as fast as I could into the house. I couldn't hear anything they were saying. There was a tall guy who seemed to be the leader who hit Kiowa over the head. I call 911 but they wouldn't get in time to stop everything. They all start jumping Kiowa, they were beating him so badly. I scream for them to stop hurting him. I knew they all were Nita, he did anything to deserve this. Kiowa was a strong guy, but seven large men, he doesn't stand a chance. As they're there beating him I feel totally helpless. I am in horror trying to figure out what I can do to get them off of him. They were all in a circle around him, I couldn't see Kiowa. The entire time I just want one cop car to show up. They all spread out amongst each other, the leader held a gun to Kiowa's head. It was crazy, I went outside. I couldn't take it any longer. They were going to kill him if I didn't do anything. My heart and brain were fighting. I choose to follow my heart.

"Stop it! We did nothing wrong! Just leave us alone." I cry out.

"Aquila, get in the house! I'm OK! I'll be in in a minute. Aquila, go in the house! Baby, please just go inside!" Kiowa struggles to say.

"Don't worry, Kiowa, we won't hurt Aquila. Aquila, don't go inside please. I want you to watch. I want you to watch me put a bullet in his brain. Ayana told us what Joe did to Taika today. Not so tough are you now!" The leader says hitting Kiowa.

"You've proven your point! Just leave!" Just as I said that I felt a pain that I have never felt before in my stomach. The pain caused me to fall to the ground.

"Aquila! Let me go!" Kiowa says watching me fall to the ground.

"You're not going anywhere. So, she's your soft spot. Aquila is the only one who can break you. Kiowa, I came here wanting to put a bullet in your head. I see now that would be too easy for you. I think we just have to kill Aquila to really cause you some pain. Let see how bad you will be hurting after we are done with her." The leader says just before the cop sirens starts.

They all get back into their cars and drive off just before the police even arrive. Covered in his own blood Kiowa couldn't just lie there without coming over to make sure I was OK. Kiowa refused to go to the hospital instead his mother comes over and examines him. I think I just got an extremely bad cramp. Koda helps Kiowa up the stairs and onto the bed. I hate that this is all my fault. Kiowa could have died tonight, there's no restart button. If there was I would have pressed it a long time ago. One of the worst things I could have done was be with Taika. I have never been so scared in my entire life. I try to get him to go to the hospital but he says that he will be fine. Ms. Maddox inspects him and surprisingly there were no broken bones. There was just swelling and bruising. I place an ice packet all over him. Luckily his mom keeps all types of medication at home just in case. She still had heavy pain killers from her back surgery. Kiowa keep dozing in and out of sleep. I couldn't sleep, I was too worried about him. I change the ice pack and gauze that was on his forehead. Even though it happened a couple of hours ago I was still shaking. When

I was done changing everything, I get up and leave. When I come back I find Ki awake trying to sit up, I tell him not to move.

I couldn't keep my hands steady. Kiowa starts moving around slowly, placing his hand on my belly and rubbing it. He just looks at me like a parent would look at their child when they're in trouble. I start crying, I know what he was going to say. A part of me didn't want to even hear it.

"Aquila, that was really dangerous for you to do! You put yourself and the baby at risk tonight! How can you do something so stupid?! You could have gotten seriously hurt and then what was I to do? What would I have done if they would have tried to kill you?!" He screams at me.

"Kiowa, I knew it was crazy for me to go out there. My heart was talking louder than my brain. I agree I shouldn't have put the baby at risk. In that moment, I completely forgot I was pregnant. I was scared and wasn't thinking." I cry.

"I would rather get the shit beaten out of me than to see anyone hurt you. I love you too much to ever put you in risk. What if the police didn't show up?! They would have hurt you and the baby! What if you would have died tonight?! What am I supposed to do without you? Do you even realize that the thought of losing you again would kill me, especially now with the baby on the way! Please don't every do that again! I mean it! I will die for you at any time if it means you will be safe." He cries.

"I'm sorry." I say.

I don't know what to do now. What the hell else could come now after all of this? Ms. Maddox and Koda want to stay the night I tell them they didn't have to. I would call them second to the police in case anything happens again.

I let them out the house and lock the house down tighter than a military base. I went to the bathroom on the main floor of the house. I was probably two steps up the stairs when there was a knock at the door. After what happened a couple hours ago I'm not opening the door for shit. I slide the drapes that were on the door to peek to see who could possibly be at the door. In utter shock I couldn't believe this asshole doesn't know how to stay away from me.

Yup, Taika's arrogant ass was at the door. As soon as she sees my face he begs me to open the door. He started doing his usual bullshit apology. I wasn't in the mood to deal with it. I walk away from the door and headed back upstairs until something he says sparks my interest.

"Aquila, I know it's hard to believe this but I never said that your baby was mine. Yes, I was upset about it. I still had hope that you would give us another chance because I owed you that. I tried to tell you at the store earlier how sorry I am but Joe showed up. They're trying to start a war. I'm not. If Ruben wasn't the only place I knew I would leave. Aquila, please open the door!"

I stop on the steps and listen to him pour his heart out. He continues. "I'm sorry about what happened to Kiowa tonight. I told Ayana what happened. She went behind my back and told the council. I'm not trying to start a war with you guys. Everyone else is trying to but they're using me to do it. I can't even trust my own sister now. Do you realize how hard that is? I'm sorry about what I said about your face. I'm sorry about your parents. Hell, I'm sorry for being the cause of all the shit you're going through right now." He says crying.

I walked back over to the door. I moved the curtain again just to see the look on his face – I could tell he was sincere. But right now it was just too much to handle. Too much has gone on in the last couple of hours.

"I'm still not opening the door. Taika this is too much for me. You have caused a lot of damage. I don't think you realize that. Kiowa and I could have died tonight. I don't know if I can trust you or not. Just go away! Taika, I told you your last apology was it for me. I'm done with you!" I say through the door.

"I'm so sorry. I never got a chance to formally apologize to you. I'll leave but you have to trust me." He continues crying and walks away.

I don't think there is anything left for me in Ruben anymore. Taika needs to stay away from me. Right now I think the only thing we can do is move. My life went downhill the night of the accident. The night I should have died, pretty sure that's were my story ended for me – especially here in Ruben. Things would be better if I wasn't around. It's been over a year, I thought I had put all the crazy shit behind me but apparently it's following me. I head back upstairs to the room and tend to Kiowa.

Like an Eagle in the Sun

Twenty five weeks and my back is killing me even the more, baby Bobbles is getting bigger and I'm really feeling her growth all in my body. Kiowa is pretty much all healed up, we haven't seen anyone form the Nita tribe. I'm hoping they continue with that. I told Kiowa what Taika said to me that night. I don't want to trust him that easily because I believe he could be very much be telling the truth. The question I have is what would be the reason behind the Nita trying to start a war again with Catori? There is something that is missing from this equation. I shouldn't be worried all the time like I am. Koda has been on winter break from school so he's been at the store watching over me. Surprisingly he hasn't complained about having to be here.

I haven't really had a chance to enjoy being pregnant. I'm terrified that someone is going to hurt me and Bobbles. There's nothing I can do if someone tries to attack me. The most disappointing thing so far is that I haven't felt the baby kick yet. My new employee is starting in the next couple of days. Bea seems very ecstatic about the job. She's in school and takes her classes at night. Bea is African American, maybe two inches taller than me, long curly brown hair. Her face was round and can be easily picked out in a crowd full of people because of her light brown eyes.

The council has been trying to gain control of the situation, they're working overtime trying to help us. I'm hoping that this will be all over with before Bobbles gets here. Every day when I'm done with the store I go home and pass out from exhaustion – mental and physical. I think that has nothing to do with Bobbles as much as it has to do with all the stress going on. I want to take some time out to focus on me and the baby. Ms. Maddox wants to take me shopping in the next couple of days. She's been trying to do everything this she can to help not be stressed out. I appreciate that from her.

Even through all of this I still have no idea what I want to name Bobbles. I can't think of a letter to start with. Her name might be Bobbles, I have no clue. Ms. Maddox also has been a lot more hands on. She is trying to help me prepare for the birth. I honestly don't think any woman can be prepared for labor no matter what. I'm pretty sure that type of pain is from another universe. I'm pretty sure I'm going to be torn apart. She's given me a ton of books to read. Which I have not even picked up considering she has two kids and is a doctor. Do I really need to read these books? I don't think so.

I hate shopping for me, but looking at things for Bobbles is more fun. Ms. Maddox finds the cutesiest things for her granddaughter. She so spoiled and she's not even here yet. It still hasn't hit me that I'm going to be a mom in the next couple of months. I still ask myself how I got here - to be such an adult at my young age. We shop, eat, and go back to my house. I need help getting out of the car now that I'm so big. I reached to unlock the door but Ki opens the door before I could. He says hi and walk passed us not looking us in the eye. I sit the bags down on the kitchen table and ask him what was wrong. Then I look over and see Taika. He was the last person I would expect Kiowa would allow himself to be in the same room with. I look at Kiowa like he was crazy, Taika's the reason for our problems.

"The hell is he doing here?" I ask in frustration.

"It's not for you to be worried about." Ki says grabbing the bags off the table.

"No! What's going on? With everything that's going on you don't get to tell me that's nothing's wrong! I have been meaning to ask what the agreement between the tribe is. I have heard stories but I don't know what exactly that all entails." I yell.

"Son?" Ms. Maddox says looking confused.

"Baby, just let me handle this." Ki says strongly.

"No, Kiowa, tell me the truth. Stop dancing around everything and just tell me." I yell.

"Ok, you know how every two months there is a meeting with both tribes. Well there is a meeting every month with just the men of the tribes. We aren't allowed to tell women the full story, because of tribal law. I'm breaking that law today. These are trade secrets you aren't supposed to know. The two tribes used to live and coexist with each other. The spirit of the bear is what they used to refer to it. Everything was going perfect. All you know about is there was a bloodbath and nearly everyone was almost wiped out. The reason the war happened was because of the Chef's daughter Julia. She was set to marry the Nita Tribe's top warrior. She refused to marry him. Turns out she was pregnant with a member of our tribe's child. They never found out who was the guy was. Somehow she comes up dead. They blamed Catori for the death of his daughter. That's when the war started. They're using us to get back at the tribe for the death of the Chef's daughter. If we weren't in different tribes none of this would be happening. Taika is telling the truth, he has no idea why they're trying to start a war now. Taika was here telling me they're coming up with a plan to attack." He says.

"Kiowa this is too much for me to be able to handle right now. We need to leave Ruben for good. We can find somewhere else to live. I feel like I have swallowed a razor blade and it slowly cutting me deeper the more I talk. We need to run away from this." I cry.

"We can't move now. It will take us too long to be able to find a house. Trust me that's the first thing I thought of. Once Bobbles is here we can try and find somewhere else to live." He grabs my hand.

If I wasn't sitting down I would have fell over. This is just simply too much for me. Kiowa helps me out of the chair and I waddled my way up to the room. I give up with trying to save myself. They might as well kill me and get it over with. The way I see it I might not even get a chance to hold my baby. Kiowa follows me to the room trying to cheer me up. I tell him to leave me alone and let me cry alone. He sits on the bed next to me and rubs my back not saying a word to me. Bobbles begins letting her mother know that everything was going to be OK, she starts kicking.

The next couple of days I stay in the house in the bed. What's the point of me trying to leave the house when someone is watching and waiting for the right moment to strike me? Being in this state has allowed me to be able start folding and putting the baby's clothes away. I didn't care about anything other than Bobbles. Focusing on her gives me the chance to forget about what was going on with the tribes. She starts kicking every time I think about it. It's her way of getting me out of my head which isn't a bad thing.

As the days go by I'm forced to leave the house because it's time for another checkup. Every time I see her during an ultrasound I feel like I'm on cloud nine. The more she grows she looks like a bobble head doll.

The nurse sets me up on the table and puts the same cold gel on my stomach. It would be nice of her if she would warm it up a bit before putting on me. She shows us Bobbles. Today she was very active moving around a lot. I was so happy until the nurse told me that she a little small for twenty five weeks. They drew blood from me to check and make sure everything was OK. My doctor came in and told us that they might put me on bedrest – I understand that it was because of all the stress that we were going through these last few weeks.

I listen to the doctor's orders because the last thing I want to do is put my baby in jeopardy. Bea had been doing a great job with the store, so I was confident that could handle everything at the store if need. I walk out of the doctor's office disappointed however, because I wasn't quite ready to walk away from the store so soon. Ms. Maddox says that there would be nothing to worry about. I leave her and Kiowa to schedule my next appointment.

Kiowa looks at me when I walk over to him after making the next appointment. I don't think most of us realize that being a parent is extremely hard. But I doubt that most soon-to-be parents don't have the threat of their lives looming over their heads. Ki and I had a lot to deal with but we were determined not to allow it to overtake us.

As Ki and I were in the car I thought we were heading home but Kiowa drives past our house. I didn't even want to ask where we were going – I submitted to whatever mission we were headed on, I was too tired to fight. We end up at the beach. Come to find out Ms. Maddox told Ki to take me on a relaxing walk to make me feel better and cheer me up. He gets out the car and walks around to my side and helps me out.

We were in the middle of winter but the waters hadn't frozen over yet. There were still waves coming onto shore. Kiowa takes my hand guiding me over along the shore. We walk along the beach holding hands. The beach has always been that one place that helps me clear my head. I feel much better about what happening right now. It's weird how everything turns around. Taika once being our enemy is now on our side trying to help us overcome the threat on our lives. Even though he sorts of really is the cause of the situation, but he can't help if someone used him to stir up an evil cause. I never thought that the two of them would be on the same side. Considering senior year they both wanted to kill each other.

We walk along the shore line, it was one of the most beautiful scenes I've seen in a long time - the beach does look beautiful in the winter. It's been a minute since I have been this relaxed. Bobbles kicks around in my stomach – it may be been because the coldness was getting to her. She was kicking so hard that Kiowa got a chance to feel her when he put his hand on the outside of my coat. We might have a soccer player on our hands as much as she likes to kick around. I realize that it would be so much that I would have to explain to her as she gets older once she was born.

When we finally made it home I prepare lunch for us. While we were eating there was a stupid reality TV show about a family who makes enough money to feed at least three continents. The doorbell rang I was going to get it, but Kiowa tells me to sit. It was Taika, he had some good and bad news to share with us. There was still some extra food left over so I offer him a plate of food. I get up and fix him a plate. Nita's head council saw that there was no harm done after everything had been explained. However, we weren't out of the clear because the Chef's son was still upset about all that had happened. The council felt that the ass whooping Kiowa took a couple weeks ago was enough to end things – for some reason that made things even. The Nita's Chef eldest son, V, is the one who started the entire war all over again. Taika tells us he believes that everything will be squashed but we just have to look out for V until everything is confirmed. V is the one who started all of the rumors – he took Taika's venting one day at one of the tribe meeting as his opportunity to start the war. But I feel somewhat reassured that everything will be OK because we now have Taika on our side. It's good to know that he wasn't lying the entire time.

I place my plate into the sink, thank Taika, and head upstairs to rest. I want to leave the two men to talk – they needed to especially after all that we've been through. I didn't expect them to be friends, but it was important that peace is established between them for once. Before heading to my bedroom, I look inside Bobbles' room. The sun was shining through her window onto her crib. Maybe her name can be Hope or Dream I think to myself as I look at the light shining in – it definitely time to make a decision because she would soon be here.

After putting the Taika situation behind us I went to the store to check up on Bea. She was doing a great job and has a wonderful personality she's been great with all the customers. It was quiet this day in the store so I decided that I was going to go in the back and do some inventory. I want to make sure that everything is all set because the baby would soon be coming and I wanted to make sure that Bea had everything she needed to run the store sufficiently while I was on leave.

As I was placing an order for inventory I hear a scream out of nowhere. I swallow hard because I can tell that Bea was in trouble. All I could think to myself is what could it be now! The office was tiny and there was not a lot of space due to the amount of paper work all over the place. I move as fast as I could before stumbling over various things in the office, but I was finally out of the office to the front. There were two male teenagers, one wearing a black mask and the other wearing a blue mask and a skullcap holding Bea at gun point. I try backing up into the office to call the police, but one of the men sees me. He instructs me to come out to the front. This is the last thing that needs to happen to me right now. I just can't catch a break. It's like one thing after the other – literally. I'm in my thoughts praying and trying to think of what we could do. I'm nearly nine months pregnant. I didn't have much fight in me for two strong men with guns.

I'm hoping that a customer would walk up to the door and see that we were being held at gun point and call the police. Bea stood in front of me in case they became even more aggressive.

"Give us all the money and I'm not playing with you!" The guy in blue says waving the gun around.

"As of lately people have been paying with their cards. Here…" Bea reaches in the register and hands him the little bit of cash we had. "All we have is $50 in cash take it and leave!" Bea says.

"I think they're lying to us. Do you think that this is a game?" The guy in black asks.

"You got what you wanted now go!" I says pushing Bea to the side of me.

"Dude, she's pregnant. We can't rob her." The one in blue says.

"We are so sorry! Here's the money back. Come on! Let's leave." The guy in black says.

In the oddest of turns my baby, Bobbles, saves the day. I couldn't help but to think that the two boys were just some young punks who didn't have the heart to go through with what they thought they had the balls to do. Bea went and locked the door while I call the police. Once the police show up they look at the surveillance footage and take it for evidence. Bea calls her girlfriend, Erica to come and pick her up. I decide to close the store for the day – we've had enough. I didn't want to tell Kiowa but I knew I had to. He drives as fast he could to me in a panicked mess.

"Quila, are you OK? Did they try and hurt you? Bea are you ok?" He says panicking.

"I'm Ok." Bea says holding Erica's hand.

"We're fine they didn't do anything. They were just two teenagers. This is the first time this has ever happened to the store. Since everyone knew that the owner's wife was a cop, no one ever dared to try something like this. Those kids must be new to the area. Hopefully this will never happen again." I say assuring Kiowa that I was fine.

"You got that right this will never happen again because I have ordered the deputies to make around the clock checkups on you two here at the store. You have been through enough and being that you are pregnant no one on the force wants to see you hurt. Even though your dad isn't here to protect you doesn't mean we won't." Officer So says.

"This robbery doesn't make any sense. This has to be there first time doing anything of this nature." Bea says.

"It really doesn't." Erica says.

"Once they saw that I was pregnant they got scared and ran off. Robber's with a moral code, I guess." I shrug my shoulders.

"Well I'm glad they had a conscious, otherwise we would be having a different conversation right now. I'm glad you both are safe." Kiowa says placing his hand on my belly.

I seem to be good a cheating death in the last year of my life. I'm not questioning it I'm just glad that nothing happened to both me and Bea today. The last thing anyone of us would want is to be gone from this world.

The next day sure enough Officer So had a squad car drive pass to make sure we were ok. Bea was working the counter while I stocked the shelves. It didn't faze her that we were held at gun point yesterday.

"Hey, Bea. How come nothing seems to bother you? You move at the beat of your own drummer." I say walking toward the front.

"I wasn't always like this. You met Erica yesterday so you know I'm gay. I like men but only on TV. In terms of someone having my heart it needs to be a woman. I was about five when I realized that there was something was wrong with me. I had a crush on this girl in my class. I kept it to myself. I figured that it would go away." She says cleaning up the counter.

"I guess it didn't." I say chuckling.

"Yeah, you're correct. Those feelings got worse once I hit seventh grade. It's not like I didn't try dating a guy. I dated this guy name Bart, but I ended that quickly. It just didn't seem right. I started dating this girl named Geovanna. I called her Geo for short. She had the most beautiful red hair I had ever seen. Anyway, Geo convinced me to tell my parents I was gay. So, I did with her right by myside. My parents freaked out. My mom sat in the corner and cried telling me I was such a disappointment. I thought it couldn't any worse than that. My dad kicked me out of the house and told me to never come back." She says.

"I'm sorry, Bea." I say feeling bad for her.

"It's perfectly fine. My grandmother took me into her home. It's already bad enough that I'm gay, but being Black and gay is much worse. One day I decide that it would be better if I wasn't around anymore. I slit both of my wrists one Sunday morning while my grandmother was at church. I lay on the bathroom floor bleeding out. I had prayed for God to not make me gay anymore. I couldn't take being shut out from my parents. I said fuck it. My grandmother came home early from church and found me on the floor. I was rushed to the hospital, later I found out if my grandmother hadn't come home early I would have been dead in an hour." She says causally.

"Bea, I don't know what to say." I respond.

"I realized that suicide doesn't solve a problem it creates a storm for the ones you love. Those who do commit suicide are the ones that don't get to see the damage that they do. Unlike many others I was given a second chance at life. A chance at actually living. Love heals all wounds. I got a second chance at life and I'm not taking it for granted. The greatest moments can come from sadness." She says as a customer walks into the store.

Bea's story was hard to hear but it was needful for me. She a lot stronger than I thought she was. It takes power being able to decide to take your own life, but it takes great strength being able to deal with your problems.

Grove of Cottonwood

I'm the size of a blue whale and I don't think I can get any bigger. It's good being that I'm in the home stretch of my pregnancy. The last seven months have been the most challenging. What I have noticed about being pregnant is that it feels like being in different body. It's worse than anything you can ever think of - the constant aches and pains. Even with everything it will all be worth it in the end. I keep going in her room and changing everything around. I just want things to be perfect when she gets here. My regular customers have been bringing in gifts for our daughter. Bea is also doing an amazing job working in the store. Her personality is good to be around because she's very down to earth and fun to be around.

Spring is coming to an end the air is starting to feel warm again. I'm having trouble sleeping at night. I have never in my life had extreme back pain like this before. Kiowa bought me this weird shaped pillow that looks like the letter "J". It's been helping me a little bit but not by much. I was still feeling tired so I left Bea in charge of the store. Kiowa took the day off to finish up the nursey for all the last minute changes that I was demanding. I was glad he was there considering I got stuck trying to get out the car he was able to help me get out of the car. I go upstairs and head for bed. It was around one in the afternoon when I arrive at the home.

I was trying to get every bit of sleep I could before Bobbles arrived. Kiowa comes and wakes me up out of my sleep – was so annoyed with him because I had finally got into a comfortable position and was getting some good sleep. I tried sitting up but got a couple of Braxton hicks in the process.

After I awake fully he's flashing a yellow dress in my face. "What's that for?" I ask wiping my eyes.

"I want you to put this on." Ki says smiling.

"For what?"

"Because I have a special surprise for you downstairs and I want you to look nice." Ki says excitedly. "Now get dressed and cleaned up and meet me downstairs."

I examine the dress initially thinking it wasn't going to fit me, but realizing that it was quite stretchy realize that it was a perfect fit. After getting cleaned up I head downstairs. As I come into view, I hear people yell out "Surprise!" Ki and Ms. Maddox

had a surprise baby shower thrown for me. I must have been

sleeping very hard because I didn't hear anyone come in nor any

commotion from all the people that were in my house. There was

so much pink around the room it looked like they killed ten-

thousand flamingos.

Lilly was dressed in pink from head to toe. The entire night

she keeps rubbing my belly and taking crazy selfies. I had fun

being the center of attention for once and for a good and joyous

reason. I would have loved for my parents to have been there with

me. Ms. Maddox was helping me open gifts when I got my first

real contraction. I start breathing through it hoping it would stop.

Kiowa and his Mom rushes to my aid. Once the contraction stops I

continue opening the many gifts. The party ends once I've opened

all of gifts. I realize that my body was preparing for delivery

because I was having sporadic contractions throughout the entire

shower. I begin to mentally prepare myself knowing that soon I'll

most likely be in full labor. I tell myself I can handle this.

And suddenly I find myself in full on labor. Ms. Maddox and Ki were putting things in the baby's room. I was sitting in the sit I was sitting in and just yell out telling everyone I was in labor.

Ms. Maddox rushes by my side to make sure that I was ok. Kiowa was calm as far as I could tell and went into full daddy mode. Koda rushes everyone out the house. Lilly starts freaking out and wants to boil water – she watches too much TV. I express to everyone that I was fine. In my head, I had no idea what I'm supposed to be doing. Everyone helps me upstairs to the room. Ms. Maddox's doctor brain started to kick in and the hippy person leaves. It was just one contraction and there all acting like my water broke. The rest of the night I lay in bed relaxing I understood that my labor pains were too far apart to prepare to go to the hospital at this point. Ki helps me onto the bed to change out of the dress.

"I have so many stenches marks it's unbelievable!" I say as I'm changing clothes.

"Those are not stretch marks and they are not bad." Ki says.

"You're only saying that because they're not on your body. What are they then if they're not stretch marks?" I say while he helps me back into bed.

"You're the tigress who has earned her stripes, and each one of them are beautiful." Ki says. He has to always look at everything so poetically.

"You have an answer for everything don't you?" I laugh and try my best to relax as it seems like the contractions have seemed to slow down. Maybe it was a false alarm.

"Yeah, I do." He smiles.

The next morning, I decide to stay home and not go into the store. Looks like the labor was a false alarm, after a few hours the contractions seemed to stop and I was feeling stable. Kiowa insisted on staying with me just in case I went into labor. I told him I would be fine and that he wouldn't know what to do anyway and that he needed to go on with his day.

"Kiowa, I'll be fine. If anything happens you will be the first one I call." I told him with my right hand placed on my belly.

"Aquila, you were having contractions last night at the baby shower. I think it's more important for me to be here than working at the hospital. I want to be there when your water breaks." He says frustrated I wouldn't let him stay.

"What if something happens at the hospital? You're an engineer they will need you. I assure you, I will be ok." I say.

"Quila?" He sighs holding on the kitchen chair.

"OK, if it will ease your mind, I will call Lilly and see if she can come over. Me and her can hang out for the day. Go to work, I will be fine. If something happens I will call you. I promise" I hand Kiowa his jacket kissing him in his cheek."

"Ok I'll go, but you call me if you even have one contraction." Then he bends down to my belly. "You be good to your mother." Ki says to my belly and kisses it before he walks out the door.

My nesting sense was starting to kick in. I couldn't stop cleaning things around the house. I can't remember the last time I have ever cleaned this much. I was scrubbing the bathroom floor when someone was knocking on the door. I say knock when really it sounds like someone was trying to break in. I looked through window of the door and it was Lilly.

"Hey, what are you doing here?" I say confused because I didn't call her.

"Kiowa called me and says to come over because he was pretty sure that you weren't going to call me." She says smiling.

"Of course, he did. Well come in." I sigh.

"Actually, I was thinking we could go to the beach for the day. This is our last time hanging out before the baby gets here. If you're still not well from yesterday we can hang out here. I just thought it would be nice for us." She says with hope.

"No, it's OK. I definitely want to go. Let me go change." I say, not really wanting to go but I do it for Lilly.

I waddled upstairs to change into the bikini I bought a while ago. Although I looked like a whale, I decide I'll have fun with it and enjoy this weather before Bobbles gets here. Lilly was of course happy being that we were going to spend the day together. She drives us to La Plano blasting her hippy music. Walking on concrete is hard enough, trying to walk on sand was even harder. We finally find a good spot and I struggle trying to get to ground. Lilly helps me sit down and then rubs my belly.

"Are you excited for her to get here? I know I am!" She says rubbing my belly again.

"Yeah, yesterday was just a reminder of what's to come." I say looking at her smiling face.

"I'm really happy for you." She looks down.

"What's with that face? You were just happy a few seconds ago. Now you look sad." I take off my sunglasses.

"I used to be jealous of you, Aquila." She says.

"What?" I respond in shock.

"Yeah. Kiowa is an awesome guy. He treats you like any girl would love to be treated. Somehow, I ended up with a jerk who has damaged me for life. You're getting married and your baby will be here soon. Even with all that has happened to you, somehow you were able to bounce back. That's why I'm jealous of you. You have an ability to bounce back easily" She says messing with her hands.

I couldn't believe that she thought I was so strong, when I was the one who took some of my inspiration and strength from a page out of her book. "Hey, what Joseph did to you was unacceptable. You are not damaged for life. It was a setback, but when you come back to you again, Lilly, you will be even stronger than you were before."

After the beach Lilly drops me off at home. Kiowa was making dinner for use, but I was so tired I went to bed. What Lilly told me at the beach early today weighed on my mind for a bit. I hope she will be OK. In fact, I know she will be, in time.

Time of the Waiting Moon

I feel like for the last nine months I have been playing baseball. I'm about to hit the biggest home run of my life. Any day she can be here in my arms lying on my chest. Mothers are the tree of life, growing strong, and when a storm hits we don't break. I have been watching other trees give birth to their branches and budding beautiful flowers. I'm very nervous about being in labor and not knowing what is going to happen. I made Kiowa watch videos with me of woman giving birth. Our daughter is going to ruin me. I don't think I will be able to look at Kiowa the same after I give birth. Really if you think about it this is all his fault. He was to be the responsible one. I can't put most of the blame on him, can I, of course I can what am I saying. I have been getting Braxton Hicks kicks pretty much every day. Knowing that I can go into labor any day, I'm trying everything you can think of to get it going. Sweet baby June, the sky is blue and I still have no idea what I'm going to call you. I have read a shit ton books with thousands of baby names in them, yet I can't find a damn name for her. Hopefully after I give birth it will come to me.

Koda volunteers to work at Waters over the summer, paid of course. Bea is still in charge, Koda is still a baby in my eyes. Plus, I have a live video surveillance at the store so I know what's going on at all times. I'm the owner of the store it doesn't even feel like I'm on maternity leave. Having me at home just waiting for the ball to drop is driving me insane.

"Hello, beautiful, let's go for a walk." Ki smiles and says.

"So now you're saying I'm fat and need exercise?" I snarl.

"No, that's not what I'm saying at all. My mom just says it can help start labor." He says trying to dig himself out of the grave he was digging.

"No need to panic, I was just messing with you. Help me up." I laugh at him.

He drives us to the beach. It was a bright sunny day and the beach was not packed. I was surprised because it was the summer time, but then again our favorite beach is never really filled with people. I waddled along the beach looking like I belong in the ocean. We walk pass a couple of families and the women would ask about the baby. Everyone is wishing us the best of luck. It won't be easy, but I know we'll be able to handle it. Millions of families before us have had babies and raised families – Ki and I will be alright. Kiowa places a blanket on the sand and helps me to the ground.

Bobbles keeps kicking around in there, I can feel her moving around. I bet it's getting tight in there so why don't you come out already is what I'm thinking as I rub my belly. I'm very eager to hold her in my arms. I'm can't sleep at night already. I wake up just thinking about her. Have you ever been so close to heaven that you can see God? That's the feeling I have when it comes to Bobbles. I would give her the last breath in my body if it meant that she would live. Kiowa sits behind me and I lay on him rubbing my belly. Looking across the ocean I was happy, I was content.

I want to give birth in the comfort of my own home. Kiowa and have turned this house, that was just a building, into a home. The idea of giving birth at home is a beautiful thing that I would like to experience. Ms. Maddox is going to help me delivery which is also comforting. I figure I'm going in labor for maybe 15-22 hours I should have the privilege to be at home. Toward the end of this pregnancy Kiowa has been getting on my last nerves. He might not make it to birth because I might kill him out of frustration. I'm just joking, but he is annoying me – I think it's the baby.

Day after day we wait for her to come. There was no sign that she was planning on coming out any time soon. It was a quiet June night and the sun had just set over the land. The moon was just starting to rise. Kiowa was rubbing my feet when we got a panicked knock at the door. Taika was yelling for us to come to the door. It sounded like an elephant was trying to break in on us. Kiowa rushes to the door and let him in.

"You guys need to leave. Like now!" He panics.

"What's going on?" Kiowa asks.

"V is going through with his plan to attack you guys. He's planning on doing it tonight, I was going to talk to the council when I heard V talking about it. I rushed over here as fast as I could." Taika says out of breath.

"What the hell is his issue? This shit was handled months ago." Kiowa says trying to figure out what to do next.

I struggle for a minute trying to stand up and get ready to leave the house. I just wanted to be left alone and live in peace. I thought this shit couldn't get any worse than what it was, but if you have been paying attention it can. I didn't even take one step when I felt it. My water broke and starts rushing down my legs. I hoped I peed on myself. I takes me a minute regain my center and calm myself. I try not freaking out because it just wasn't the time to be tripping. Let me just say that Bobbles has perfect timing. I wanted her here but not when I might die before hand.

"Ok, Quil. We have to leave now." Ki starts panicking.

"We can't leave Kiowa." I say calmly.

"Quil, we can't argue about this now we have to go. We need to try and find somewhere safe." He insists.

"Kiowa, my water just broke we can't leave. Oh my, God. I'm in labor! The baby is coming! What are we going to do? What am I supposed to be doing right now?" I start freaking out I can't help it.

"You have got to be kidding me right now." He rubs his head.

"What in the hell are we going to do now?" Taika says.

Kiowa stood there in shock for a minute. He soon snaps out of it and realized that there is no way we can leave. Kiowa rushes to my aid and helps me sit down. They both start talking to me but I had gone deaf for a minute. The pains of labor start to kick in. No longer was I able to make any decisions. My body was preparing to bring life in the world. Kiowa quickly called his mom over. I can do this, I can do this I say to myself repeatedly to help me focus. It wasn't working though, I start crying because I was fearful. I realize that I wasn't in control and I didn't have all the answers. Giving birth is one of those situations which I can't control. Kiowa tries to calm me down but he couldn't, there was another human being getting ready to come out of me. I'm about to be ripped apart.

I have never been in this much pain in my entire life. I would rather have every bone in my body broken over and over than to be in labor. Ms. Maddox finally made her way to our house to help me through the labor. Kiowa, Taika, Casey, Joe, and Koda were trying to deal with the V situation. While I lie in bed wanting to die. Ms. Maddox was trying to coach me through the contractions. I was a complete mess and couldn't stop crying. Listen there is nothing that can do to really prepare yourself to be in this type of pain. You're just going to have to lay there and suffer. You know, I claim to be a self-proclaimed feminist and I happy that we can do the work of men and bear the babies, too. But I must admit, after experiencing it, I wish men could take part in the labor as well. They help make the baby so they should feel some of the pain as well.

It was weird having Taika there helping with all of this. He is my ex who for some reason we can't get away from each other. Kiowa was jumping around the house trying to keep everything organized. There are no books on how to be in labor, while someone tries to kill you. As the hours rolled on the pain gets worse and worse. Each time I get a contraction the pain goes deeper and deeper within me. Kiowa called the council and makes them aware of what is going on. There's nothing we can do if V decides to go through and attack us tonight.

There is both life and death surrounding us right now. Kiowa was doing everything he could to try and keep me calm. He massages my back and tries giving words of encouragement to me.

Ms. Maddox checks to see how far I had dilated. She starts talking

about how both labors went with her boys. She was trying to give

me some last minute motherly advice. I couldn't thank her enough

for all she has done and will continue to do for me. She has helped

me heal through the car crash, being drugged, and now birth. There

is nothing I can do to repay her for what she has done for me. I

didn't want this many people to watch me bring Bobbles into the

world. They all don't have to be here risking their lives for me. I

shuffled around the house trying to keep my energy up. Everyone

just looks at me, almost like they felt bad. All the guys were

huddled in a corner, scared for their life. While Ms. Maddox helps

me through labor I couldn't help but scream and cry when I got a

contraction.

It's one in the morning and not a single person has slept.

I'm sure most of it is mainly because I was screaming in pain from

the contractions. Ms. Maddox and Kiowa were doing everything to

try and help me along. There's is only so much that everyone could

do. She instructs me to roll on to my back, it's time for here to check my cervix again. Ms. Maddox puts on a glove and sticks a couple of her fingers inside to check.

"Good news, Aquila, your agony will be ending soon. It will most likely be another hour or so and then you will need to start pushing. Hopefully she moves faster than that and makes her way into this world. I will be so elated because then both of my babies will have a baby." She smiles removing the gloves walking out the room.

"I'm so proud of you." Ki says helping at my side.

"For what? I feel like I'm going to die. You're lucky if we try to have a son." I say while getting a contraction.

"For always being there for me. From the time when we were kids you were someone I could always go to. You have always been the one person I could always count on. If someone were to tell me that one day I would be so lucky to have you as my wife and for you to be the one to bear my child. I would have told them they're crazy. She could never love me the way I love her. I would have never thought we would be in this moment together." Ki says holding me.

"Kiowa, I love you." I say breathing through a contraction.

Koda and Ms. Maddox come rushing into the room like the house was on fire.

"Kiowa, V is outside. He has a shit ton of people out there." Koda says freaking out.

"I can't leave, Quil! Any minute now she has to start pushing." Ki says looking at me.

"Kiowa, go I'll be OK. I'll hold off as long as I can. We have at least two hours before she needs to push." I say.

"I will watch her, son." Ms. Maddox says.

Kiowa kisses my forehead not wanting to leave me and ran downstairs. Ms. Maddox ensures me that everything will work out. In the back of my head I completely doubt her. She holds my hand and we both wait.

Why the hell is V here? I think to myself. I can have the baby any minute now and he is ruining my birth experience. This is the last thing we need right now. Ms. Maddox grabs the phone to call the council. They are the only ones who could stop this. Kiowa steps outside confident that this could all blow over smoothly. I just want all of this to be over right now.

"You have no business being over here." Kiowa says with confidence as they hear me screaming in the background.

"That must be sweet. Little sweet, Aquila is in labor. Look boys, someone's going to be a dad, but he may also might be a dead dad and never get a chance to see his baby." V laughs spitting on the ground.

"V, why don't you leave? Let them be in peace. Aquila doesn't need this right now." Taika says.

"Taika since when are you on Kiowa's side? The bitch has you sprung and she doesn't even want you." V says.

"Watch your mouth when you address my wife." Kiowa starts to walk down the stairs.

"Look, I don't want to make you upset. I'm sorry I called her a bitch. I really meant you." He snarls.

"Why are you doing this, V? The elders have already spoken." Taika asks.

"Why are you helping them Taika? You have told me a hundred times Kiowa has always been interfering with your

relationship when you were with her. You should be on our side!"
He yells.

"That's only because I'm jealous of Kiowa. I put Aquila through hell being with her. Kiowa can do something I can't seem to figure out. He knows how to treat the woman he loves right. It's because of my mother I will never be able to love another woman, mine was too busy sleeping with everyone and getting high. The only reason I didn't like Kiowa was because he was able to be a man. I still do love Aquila, but I will never have her heart. I can't love a woman until I get help and fix my problems. If I'm going to do anything right in my life I'm going to help make sure she is safe tonight." Taika yells.

"Why are you doing this?" Joe asks.

"You want to know why? The reason is because all those years ago your people kill Julia and ruin everything for us. We had money, power, we had it all. Now we are stuck with this shitty piece of land and are poor because of you guys. I have been trying to come up with a plan for year. Once I heard about your little problem with Taika I knew that this was my chance to get back at the Catori Tribe. Sure, this won't make up for what your people did, but it will make me feel better." V says pissed.

"That had nothing to do with us. I can't make up for something that happened many years ago. No one knows how she died. You're completely fucking insane. No matter what tribe we're in we are all still Native. The blood of our ancestors still runs through our veins. We all have the same struggle no matter what! You're taking this too far." Ki says.

Ms. Maddox and I wait for a while without hearing a word from anyone. I want to know did they kill each other because all the shouting had stopped. I try to be strong for my baby but I was concerned if the men were going to make it through. My contractions were getting closer and closer together. She was going to be here any minute now. I'm trying to hold her in so that Kiowa wouldn't miss the birth. I look at Ms. Maddox for comfort because I didn't know what the hell was going to happen.

"Aquila, I'll be right back." Ms. Maddox says but I can tell she was very scared.

As I lie there in the bed unable to focus on what going with me and the baby. I do everything I can to fight the urge to push. I'm a tree that is done growing her flower. I couldn't help but cry not knowing what was going to happen. My body aches wanting to gain some relief I just ask God to hear my prayer.

"God, it's me again. I don't know what your plan is for me here in this moment. I just want you to remember the deal we made a while ago. Hopefully you still remember what we talked about. My old life is over, this new one that I'm about to bring into the world is all I want you to focus on. Whatever happens tonight I'm at peace with it." I pray and hold onto my stomach.

It's a good thing I was busy upstairs focusing on the baby because outside was a mad house. They were all slamming each other into the ground like animals. I could hear Ms. Maddox yelling at everyone to stop it. One of the young men tries to get into the house. Ms. Maddox is blocking him, but it took all her strength to push him down the stairs. Her granddaughter was about to be born into the world and her mother bear strength came out.

"That is enough! All of you!" Councilman Xzavier fires a gun shot.

"Kiowa? Ms. Maddox?" I scream.

"Vincent, I'm so disappointed in you. My son, you have lied to me and to the council. This is not who we are. We are not violent people, we can never forget our history, but we will not repeat it. I have made arrangements for you to be committed to an intuition out of town." He says.

"All of you who are Nita are to get back in your cars and head home. We will discuss in the morning your punishment. Kiowa, we are sorry to you and to your family. We have issued out a new order that places you and your family under the protection of the council. I suggest you all go home now." Councilwoman Gina says who accompanied Councilman Xzavier.

"Dad!" V yells.

"Don't you *dad me!* Now get in the car!" He yells.

"Goodnight everyone." He says.

Kiowa races in the house upstairs to see me crying and screaming for help. I could no longer stand the pain of as Bobbles moves her way in my birth canal. Our baby was ready to be born into the world and I was not able to stop it.

"Aquila!" Ki races up the stairs.

"Kiowa, I need to push! I need to get her out of me now!" I cry.

"Mom!" Kiowa yells.

I was completely exhausted beyond all belief. I was so close to giving up. I push hard feeling her head and shoulders completely tear me apart. I couldn't help but scream in pain. I push not knowing what was to come of the future. I push knowing that my old life was ended and my new life was beginning. While pushing her out I relived all the good and bad memories of the last year of my life. In this moment, I realize that today starts my new life. I push until I heard her, my daughter. I hadn't seen her face only her slimy body. Ms. Maddox wraps her into a towel. There was a sleepy feeling that had come over me. I try to keep my eyes open but they fell heavy.

I pass out on the bed, Ms. Maddox handed the baby over to Koda who takes her out the room. Ki didn't even get a chance to hold his baby because the love of his life was losing consciousness. I was losing a lot of blood. Ms. Maddox discovers that I was suffering from a blood hemorrhage. She struggles to stop the bleeding. She orders someone to call an ambulance and for them to hurry. Kiowa holds me unconscious in his arms crying hoping that I would wake up. Everyone is watching unsure what to do and what to say.

I end up being in a white room with nothing in it. I search trying to find someone. None of this makes any sense to me. Where am I?

"Aquila, dear?" I hear my mom's voice. I look around trying to find her.

"Mom?! Dad?! Where am I?" I ask unsure of where I was.

"Sweetie, calm down. You're somewhat dead. They call this the transition period, you're dead but not completely dead." She says.

"What? So I'm in heaven? I need to get back! My daughter, what about my baby? I didn't even get a chance to hold her! I can't leave her!" I yell.

"Calm down you're not staying." I hear my dad's voice. It was very angelic. "You have nothing to be worried about. You will see her soon enough just breath. God is giving us a chance to fix our mistakes. We wanted to say that we love you. We both don't

want you to harp over our death anymore. That night a lot of things

were said. We want you to forgive us for what we have done to

you. Your mother and I didn't realize how much we made you

suffer through with our fighting. We forgive you, and hope you

forgive us." He cries.

"You would be pleased to know that we do not fight

anymore." My mother chimes in to reassure all that my dad has

said. "We have worked out our issues. We wished that it wouldn't

have taken death to do so. I know that you will be an amazing

mother and wife. I'm so proud of you and all that you have done!

Out of all the people in the world, who would have thought Kiowa

would be the one. Just yesterday you guys were kids playing in the

mud. Now you two are parents!" She cries hugging me.

I couldn't believe that this was happening. All that I had

been through and God thought enough of me to allow my parents

to officially say good bye to me. "Of course I forgive you. I love

you both. Dad, I forgive you and I want you to know I love you no

matter what. Mommy, I love you so much! I don't think you know how much I miss you guys!" I cry some more hugging the both of them.

"Now you go back and be an amazing mother. All is forgiven, we will always be with you and your family no matter what." My mother says holding my face whipping my tears away.

It was the midday the next day and I awaken in the hospital by the sound of my child crying with Kiowa holding her in his arms. I woke up and just looked at the family that I created all on my own.

"Kiowa that is the most beautiful thing I have ever woken up to." I say smiling trying to sit up.

"Be careful don't move so fast." Ki looks at the baby girls and starts talking baby talk. "What's that? You want to see your mommy? You do?" He hands her over to me and I reach out and grab her.

"Hello little one. I'm your mother. I have been waiting for you for so long. Your eyes are bright like fire opal in the light. You are so beautiful, I didn't know I could create such a beautiful thing." I smile staring down at my daughter.

My daughter was wrapped in a yellow blanket. She has the most beautiful chubby cheeks I have ever seen in the world. She keeps opening and closing her eyes to look at me as I talk to her. I have never seen a prettier baby than her. My life is now completed with her in it. Ms. Maddox walks in the room with balloons and flowers. She was wearing a shirt that said, *best grandmother in the world.* I think it's safe to say she's enjoying being a grandmother so far.

"Look who is awake! Congrats, my dear, she is such a dream. I'm so proud of the both of you. Aquila, she looks just like you. Kiowa stand next to Aquila this is you guys' first family photo." Ms. Maddox takes a picture of the three of us.

"Quil, about last night." I cut him off.

"Ki, I don't care about anything other than her right now. Everything else doesn't matters other than her. I'll go through it all over again if it means that we will have her." I cry holding my beautiful baby girl.

"So what's the name?" He asks.

"Opal." She says.

"Opal?" He questions.

"Yeah, Opal Mitena Maddox. Her eye is like a rare fire opal stone and not one is like it." I reply looking at Kiowa. He looks down at our daughter and smile.

"Well welcome to the world little Opal Mitena Maddox." He smiles again.

Valley of Flowers

This time leaving the hospital I feel sure of my purpose of life. My daughter Opal will live a normal life with both her parents loving each other. Whether I died or not I'm happy that I got to talk to my parents. I had never yelled at them before in my life. I would have never thought that the first time I would ever raise my voice at them would be the last time I would ever talk to them in this lifetime. The accident gave me time to heal not physically, but deep within my soul. Only God knows what would have happen if they didn't die in that crash. I would most likely be in the same shit hole. I might not have fell in love with Kiowa either, which means we wouldn't have created Opal.

The only thing I want to do now is care for Opal. She has so many people that will watch her grow and to become a woman. Opal doesn't know yet how much I truly care for her. I'm lucky to have her here in my life for the rest of my life. The drive home from the hospital was short. I look at her the entire way home kissing her little hand. I can't believe I'm really a mom now. I catch a glimpse of Kiowa in the mirror looking at me.

"I will love you forever." I say rubbing her face.

We arrive at the house with Ms. Maddox waving her hand like a monkey waiting on us. I was tired and wanted to go to sleep before Opal woke up as she had fallen asleep in the car on the drive home. Ms. Maddox helped me out the car and I carried Opal into the house.

When I get into the house I see too many people at the house that I wasn't planning on seeing. "What's going on?" I say looking strangely.

"Well we think no day is better than to have your wedding today. Ki and I planned to marry you all today." She says happily. I couldn't do anything but shake my head, Ms. Maddox is always planning something.

"Ms. Maddox I don't think we are really up for a wedding." I say not knowing what to do.

"Mom, she just had the baby let her rest. It might have been a bad idea. I didn't think it all through." Kiowa says trying to reason with his mother.

Lilly was in on the wedding too, I'm shocked she could keep it in that long. She hands Kiowa a tux and instruct him to go to La Plano beach. I watch Ms. Maddox rush Kiowa into the car sending him away. I was completely caught off guard. Ms. Maddox is insane but I know she means well. Opal doesn't realize she has one crazy grandmother. My stomach hadn't gone back down over night and she wants me to put on a wedding dress. Let's not forget that I'm still trying to recover from child birth.

"Ms. Maddox, I just had her. She doesn't need to be out like this. I'm still very swollen." I try to explain to her.

"Yes and since you have the sweetest baby in the world, you and my son are meant to be together. It's the perfect time. Now come on let's get you two inside and ready." She says looking at me and Opal.

She had a team of makeup, hair-stylist there waiting to for me at the house. The dress she picks out was the perfect size considering I had just given birth. Ms. Maddox manages to get a custom wedding dress in three days. The dress was strapless white gown with blue airbrushed into it. The dress was decorated with rhinestones going across the bust. Ms. Maddox and Lilly help me into the dress. I decide not to put on the vail. I spent a year trying

to hide my scares, why hide them now on my wedding day,

especially since this is the part of me that Kiowa loves the most. I

walk down the stairs and everyone just looks at me and says how

beautiful I was. Ms. Maddox puts Opal in a white onesie with blue

gym shoes on. In the center of the shoes she places a fake opal

stones on them. My poor baby just wanted to sleep and not have to

be dressed up for her parents' wedding. Just before we were about

to leave Taika shows up at the door.

"Hey, Taika." I say bouncing Opal back to sleep.

"Hey, I wanted to see you and the wedding before I left

town. You look beautiful by the way. Again, sorry for everything."

He says placing his bag on the step.

"You knew about the wedding?" I ask.

"The whole town does I think." He laughs.

"Well, I need to apologize to you. I'm sorry for not trusting

you when you were telling the truth. Also for shutting you out

when I got into the accident. I also want to thank you for helping me while I was in labor. You didn't have to do that." I say smiling at him.

"Shit, I never thought I would earn your trust again. Sorry, I shouldn't swear in front of…" He says stopping as he wonders what my daughter's name is.

"Opal." I say smiling.

"That's a beautiful name." He smirks looking at Opal.

"Well I should get going I don't want to miss my train, and you don't want to miss your wedding. I need to find my piece of happiness." He says picking his bags up.

"Come on, Aquila we don't want to be late for your wedding." Lilly says rushing me down the stairs.

Ms. Maddox drives all of us to the beach and there are flowers and candles everywhere. There were so many of our friends and family there I didn't understand how she was able to do this in a short amount of time. Ms. Maddox screams, "Here comes Aquila!" As I walk down the beach with Opal instead of a bouquet flowers. No one had seen her other than us. Everyone was in awe of my daughter. I reach what I guess is now my soon to be husband at the altar. He is smiling from ear to ear.

"Your mother is insane." I say.

"Tell me something I don't know." He laughs.

"Dearly beloved we are gathered here today to celebrate the holy matrimony of Kiowa Maddox and Aquila Waters. If anyone doesn't agree with this matrimony speak now or forever hold your peace." Everyone stops for a moment and looking around. There are no objections. "Now will the couple like to say their vowels?" The pastor continues.

I look at Kiowa I'm sort of speechless because I didn't know I was getting married today. Opal starts crying and I am slightly embarrasses as I stand in front of everyone trying to calm a newborn down as a new mom. I bounce around patting her on her butt hoping she would go back to sleep. I couldn't help but look at her, it's kind of hard being born into the world and expected to be the flower girl. She calms down and I make Kiowa go first.

"Although this was quick and put together at the last minute, I know exactly what I want to say to my bride. What I'm about to say is truly coming from the heart. Aquila, I can't express to you how much I truly care for you. I love you more than the air I breathe. I don't know how I was able to find the only red diamond in the entire world, but I'm glad I was able to. From this point on I will get to wake up every day knowing I got to marry my best friend and create this beautiful child. I can think back to every important moment in my life and you're in every single moment. Opal truly has an amazing mother. I hope she grows up to be just like you. You're one of the most amazing people I could have ever met. I can't wait to spend the rest of my days with you. I love you." He says with tears rolling down his face.

I'm crying as well as I become overcome with love from my groom. "Kiowa, you are the reason why I tell my heart be still. Around you I get this feeling that the world could come crashing down and I wouldn't care because I have you holding me. You have been with me from the time we were kids. I'm glad to know that you're not going anywhere. When the accident happened, lost my parents, and my face was destroyed you never left my side helping me get through the last two years. I can't image what my life would be like if we weren't together. You have given me so much, I never really got to thank you for all you have done for me. Opal is lucky to have you as a father. You are strong, funny, and caring. I love you and I'm happy to be Mrs. Maddox." I say with the biggest smile on my face.

"It gives me great honor to present to you all Mr. and Mrs. Maddox. You may now kiss the bride and live forever in happiness." The pastor says.

Kiowa kisses me and I look him straight in his eyes. Opal was sound asleep in my arms. I guess I truly found heaven on earth. Even with everything that has happened to me I wouldn't change it.

"Till death do us part." I say laughing.

"Even in death I could never leave you." Ki says smiling.

We walk down the beach together not just as one, but as a family.

About the author

I am Aisha Buford-Morrison, a 19-year-old African American woman from the South Side of Chicago. I graduated from Epic Academy Charter High School in 2016. *Heart Be Still* is one of the greatest accomplishments I could have ever dreamt of. I would have never thought that at 19 I would have self-published my own book. When I was little I would always write short stories. I would have never imagined that one day I would have a book of my own. *Heart Be Still* is something that I will always hold dear to my heart. I am Aisha Buford-Morrison, enjoy reading my book.

www.ingramcontent.com/pod-product-compliance
Lightning Source LLC
Chambersburg PA
CBHW061547170626
46811CB00001B/114